D0331137

Bringing Back the Dead

BRINGING BACK
THE DEAD

JOE DOMENICI

THOMAS DUNNE BOOKS

ST. MARTIN'S PRESS ⚹ NEW YORK

THOMAS DUNNE BOOKS.
An imprint of St. Martin's Press.

BRINGING BACK THE DEAD. Copyright © 2008 by Joe Domenici. All rights reserved. Printed in the United States of America. For information, address St. Martin's Press, 175 Fifth Avenue, New York, N.Y. 10010.

www.thomasdunnebooks.com
www.stmartins.com

Book design by Richard Oriolo

Library of Congress Cataloging-in-Publication Data

Domenici, Joe.
    Bringing back the dead / Joe Domenici.—1st ed.
        p.   cm.
    ISBN-13: 978-0-312-38046-5 (alk. paper)
    ISBN-10: 0-312-38046-1 (alk. paper)
    1. Vietnam War, 1961–1975—Veterans—Fiction.   2. Vietnam War, 1961–1975—Psychological aspects—Fiction.   I. Title.
PS3604.O455B75   2008
813'.6—dc22   2008021473

First Edition: September 2008

10   9   8   7   6   5   4   3   2   1

For my sister Cindy,
without whom this would have been impossible to write

And for those who served

ACKNOWLEDGMENTS

No book is written in a vacuum. There are many people to thank here.

First, thanks to Larry Yoder, who allowed me the use of his name and parts of his history. Also to Fred Custer, who did the same, and who tolerated many afternoon talks informing me about the U.S. Special Forces training in the early seventies and his Vietnam experiences.

To the City of Belle Glade, Florida, I offer my sincere apologies. I have been to your fair streets. My book does not do justice to them. But a book needs a villain, so I created "Poppa" Cole and his offspring. As far as I know, there are no Coles in Belle Glade; if there are, they have my apologies, and the reader should not confuse them with my fictional creations.

Thanks go to Jim Riggs, who tried to keep my air force and airplane information honest. David Hargis gave me a love of Townes Van Zandt and tolerated my refusal to let royalty enter the book. Henry Schaffer deserves thanks for handing me Walter Wager's 58 *Minutes* years ago. Marcy Troy vetted the raw manuscript, and so I give thanks to her. Tom Wellman also read it early on and gave solid input and corrections.

Thanks to David Powell, president of the 1/92nd FAA, C Battery, '70–'71, of BraveCannons.org, who saved me the embarrassment of a major error on the 155mm guns. BraveCannons.org is a great Web site.

To "Sharkey," who allowed the poor imitation of the real man and also vetted the raw manuscript for military errors. A large thanks to Sherry Evans, who spent weeks doing grammar corrections and checked the raw manuscript for errors.

Joe Lansdale deserves a special note here. He told me how to just plow on through to the next section when I became stalled. I would also like to acknowledge Stephen King's *On Writing*. It helped give me some of the tools of writing from a master's toolbox. Pat Conroy's *My Losing Season* deserves mention also. That book taught me that I should write. Thomas F. Monteleone deserves special credit for helping a young author in a writers' workshop at a World Fantasy Convention long ago. He does not remember me, but I do remember him.

Thanks also to my editors, Tom Dunne and John Schoenfelder, who took a chance. A special thanks to India Cooper, who performed the herculean task of copyediting and correcting the manuscript.

Any errors, technical or geographic, are the fault of the author and no one else.

A PAST NIGHT

CHAPTER 1

Never take both boots off at the same time.

—POI 7658 Special Forces Combat Manual ROV 1970

VIETNAM—JANUARY 1973

NO ONE WANTED TO BE OUT here. Not the six U.S. Special Forces soldiers or their Vietnamese guide, Mr. Pham. Not the NVA or the Viet Cong or the Cambodians they were trying to evade. Even the jungle animals were restless that night, as they sensed there was no point to roaming under that jungle canopy at midnight. Not that night.

The tiger that padded noiselessly across the jungle floor one hundred yards from the Americans did not feel good about the night. Mr. Pham sensed the tiger, but said nothing to the Americans.

Most Americans did not understand the tiger, so Mr. Pham was silent. He did not know that he was not alone in sensing the tiger's presence.

The end of the war was coming, the war machine slowing down. Everyone knew that, and no one wanted to be the one who took *the* final bullet a day before it all ended.

The Christmas Bombings had brought the North Vietnamese running back to the peace table in Paris. The message was clear from the White House, and there are few things as convincing as a few tons of well-placed Arc Light. Nixon had hammered the enemy with everything he had for twelve days. Hanoi got the message and returned to the talks. The war would finally grind to a stop, but before that there were loose ends to clean up. Missions were still being assigned.

Grade A intel had come through to Saigon. Grade A meant that it came from Americans in the field. There was a POW camp about thirty klicks on the other side of the Cambodian border. That was definite bandit territory in a land where bad things happened.

The intel said that there were Americans being held there, and Saigon wanted, for once, to free some POWs—a redemption of all the bad with at least one good mission. Everyone wanted a clean wash in cool, clear water to purge his soul, if only for a moment, of this rotten war. No one wanted to go home a total loser.

The intel came into Saigon, and reports were written and sent up the line. Generals conferred and sent definite orders back down. If this was real, find the camp. They wanted confirmation. If it checked out, they would launch a rescue mission and free those men. So REMF majors and palace-dog colonels in air-conditioned offices formed the data into orders. This was a strange art form using typed words instead of clay or paint. The canvas was the grasslands and jungles in Vietnam, Laos, and Cambodia. Those orders became moving flesh, steel, and lead. Pointless battles were fought and lives were lost, but orders were orders, so someone had to go. Men were chosen. The generals asked for the best A-Team Special Forces had in-country, and they got Captain Fred Custer and his men.

CUSTER WAS SITTING IN HIS command post at Firebase Nancy, next to the tiny hamlet of Dok Hon in the Kontum district, when a Huey came in with the orders. He was planning a minor operation into Laos "just to fuck with" the VC supply lines. It was something to do, and he was tired of the constant flow of RPGs and AKs that generally made his life more difficult and certainly more dangerous. He wanted a little breathing room. Since the B-52s were all assigned up north or taking a rest, he figured it was time to take a little initiative. Old Victor Charlie was getting a little too confident in Custer's area. It was Custer's area as long as he was stationed here. He, his men, and their Montagnards would keep it that way. The "Yards," a nickname the Green Berets gave the mountain tribal soldiers, were fine troops.

Custer had joined the army in 1962, after John F. Kennedy's famous speech at Fort Bragg that brought attention to the then unknown Special Forces Green Beret units. Inspired by JFK's Camelot and the Special Forces, Custer worked hard and became one of those elite men. He was one of the first advisers into the mountains of Vietnam, and he was in his third tour in a country he had come to love.

In the field, Custer carried the CAR-15 as his main rifle. He liked the shorter barrel length and lighter weight of the carbine better than that of the AR-15. He had the division gunsmith burr the chamber and ramp it down until the weapon did not jam. With his rifle and the usual hand grenades and claymores they all carried, Fred toted the ever trusty Colt .45 pistol on his hip for backup.

Custer barely even heard the chopper blades cutting through the air when the Huey arrived with his new orders. Chopper noise had become second nature to him long ago. It wasn't a threat, so his mind set it aside. After a few minutes Mac, the fire-base Top, entered Custer's command post. This was really just four walls of sandbags with a tin roof, one desk, one chair, and military maps pinned on the walls. Mac stood in front of the desk, silent.

Fred Custer liked Mac. He was a good sergeant and a better soldier, having started in the frozen hell of Korea. Mac had worked his way up the line from buck private to first sergeant. It may have been a captain's official role as base commander, but everyone knew that it was Top Mac who really ran the camp.

His last name was MacDonald, but everyone just called him Mac. The troops all liked him. He was as tough as they came, but he had seen the shit and they knew it, and he had never forgotten his buck private days. He knew what it was like to throw lead and have it thrown back at you. Mac took care of his men.

Custer leaned back, pushing his gold-rimmed glasses up the bridge of his nose, and pulled a Marlboro from its pack and lit it with his 82nd Airborne Zippo.

"What do we have going on, Mac?" he asked, blowing smoke out like a dragon testing his breath. He knew that if Mac came to him something was up.

"Not we, Fred. You. You and your little Boy Scout troop are going on a field trip." Mac tossed the orders across the top of the desk where Custer was plotting out his route into Laos. "Hell, you guys must have impressed some Scout leader at national head-quarters. Or you really pissed someone off. You're going deep into Cambodia."

Custer crushed his cigarette out and picked up the orders to read them.

"Yeah, sorry to say your little trip to Laos is postponed. That's a good idea," Mac said, as he picked up Custer's cigarette pack and lit one. The only time Mac smoked was when he was out of his HQ, and that was not often. Mac rotated the map around on the desktop so that it faced him. "Who knows, I just may take a few men and go out there myself. I sit behind that desk too much. Maybe time to kick a little NVA ass in person. Maybe I'll catch General Giap himself."

Custer read through the pages a second time before speaking.

"Why us? There have to be teams down there in Quang Duc who know the territory better."

"Ours is not to question why," Mac answered. "But this is ASAP. And it comes from top brass. The chopper that brought the orders is waiting for you and your team. You have thirty minutes. Good luck. Write if you can, and don't forget to pack a lunch."

Mac smiled, dropped his cigarette to the ground, and crushed it under the heel of his boot. He turned to leave, then thought a second and faced Custer again.

"I'll send some smoke signals down the lines. I still know a couple of old bastards like me down in that area. I'll get you frequencies to some 155s that you can call in if the Girl Scouts over there get too mean." Mac turned and walked out, his final words coming as he stooped under the sandbagged entrance.

"I hear they have some mean Girl Scouts in Cambodia. Watch your ass, Custer. Don't be like your namesake."

Like all Special Forces men, Custer could be ready to go in five minutes tops. The thirty minutes Mac had given his team was a luxury. He was out of his CP in a flash and over to Sergeant Ted Hickman of the team. Hickman was young, far too young, but then so were a lot of the boys over here. However, Hickman was good. He was a natural soldier who had gravitated to Special Forces as many did—from rebellion.

Hickman stood like some bronzed Norse god at six foot three and weighed a lean, muscled 210 pounds. His blond hair was cut close with a flat top above his blue eyes and his hawk nose. Beads of sweat rolled across his bare chest. He sat checking a run of 7.62 mm ammo fresh from an ammo box, one round at a time. It was his ass on the line, and he liked to double-check things.

Born in a tough part of a borough of New York City in 1953,

by eighteen he was a rough kid of the streets, where he honed his skills. A natural leader, he led a gang. The summer after he graduated from high school, he had gone too far one night when he took down an off-duty cop. The cop had hit on Hickman's girlfriend, and Hickey—a nickname of the streets that had stuck—had beaten the man badly.

The cop even had the first punch in the row, but Hickey was a savage street fighter: The officer would be finishing his years on the force behind a desk, after his new teeth came in and his back healed. The judge had given Hickey a choice—jail or the military. His mother had cried, and his father, who had long since lost any control over Hickey, hoped the army would straighten the boy out.

Once in boot camp, his rebel side hardly conquered, Hickey saw other renegades watching from afar as he ran and did push-ups for the drill instructors. These men all seemed to wear Ray-Ban sunglasses, and even in their army uniforms they looked to Hickey like James Dean. They stood alone or in small groups, watching with amusement as the new men did their drills. Hickey studied these men with envy and found out that they were Special Forces—they had all earned the coveted Green Beret.

Hickey talked to his drill sergeant, who told him that any soldier could try out for the Special Forces after he completed his basic training. Since it was 1971, it was uncertain whether Hickey would be going to Vietnam. If he *was* going to the land of bad things, Hickey didn't want to go with just the six weeks of training that boot camp gave. He wanted to survive. The best way to do that was through training, and the best training in the army was the Special Forces. That, plus the naturally rebellious nature of many of the Special Forces men, drew Hickey to them.

After boot camp he applied and got his chance to earn the coveted Green Beret. He went off to Advanced Infantry Training and jump school at Fort Benning, Georgia, in the sweltering southern heat. There he earned his jump wings. Then he was off to the home of the Green Berets, Fort Bragg, North Carolina, where the tests really began.

The physical tasks never even slowed him down. He was a natural athlete and liked a challenge, but for an underschooled boy of eighteen, the massive book work was a chore, so Hickey pushed himself and plowed through the material. He barely passed, but he did pass. He earned that beret. Then it was time for the real training.

The once standard one year of training for the Green Berets had been cut to six months by the time Hickey went through it. The Vietnam War was still demanding bodies. At Bragg they trained in weapons, explosives, counterinsurgency, jungle warfare, jungle survival, platoon tactics, radios, medical and first aid, lessons in Vietnamese, and more. The old-timers knew that it was not enough training or time, but was there ever enough before a war?

They were up at 5:00 A.M. every morning to start the day with a ten-mile run, humping a field pack full of rocks. He and his fellow freshmen were pushed and pushed hard until well past midnight. This was a further weeding-out process, and in the end, those who remained were the best that the U.S. Army produced. These best were then sent to a five-week course nicknamed "Tiger Land" at Fort Polk, Louisiana. Tiger Land had been built and was run by men who had survived Vietnam, and these men were trying their best to make sure the young freshmen would also return home. After graduating, the young troops were shipped off to Vietnam to be tested against a fine fighting army.

The Viet Cong—Victor Charles—had begun their fight with the Japanese in World War II. Then they took it to the French for another decade. In 1954, the VC had won after General Giap cornered and destroyed the French on a little mountain in northwest Vietnam called Dien Bien Phu.

That had brought the Americans rolling in. Some of the Viet Cong were twenty-year veterans by that time, and all were to be respected as fighters. The Viet Cong played defense by taunting, evading, and teasing the American forces until 1968. That year, during the New Year Tet holidays, Victor Charlie surprised everyone with a massive offensive across all of Vietnam. The VC were beaten back, but not without major casualities on both sides. Both had suffered deep losses in men and in politics.

After the '68 Tet offensive, the American home front was never the same; the tide had turned. This was the beginning of the end for the American forces in Vietnam, but the VC had also destroyed itself in that attack. They were decimated, and the Communist leaders in Hanoi and China took full advantage. The North Vietnamese Army took over the war. Born much more out of Communist Chinese ideology than the freedom fighter base of the VC, the NVA were professional, well armed, and well equipped. They trained hard, and they upped the ante on the U.S. forces. So men like Hickey were sent to do battle. Ted Hickman loved a fight.

Custer kicked the dry red dust of the Vietnamese countryside up into the air as he walked over to Hickey. Hickey would get the rest of the team together. Although the sergeant had been only eighteen when he arrived, Custer had become impressed with his natural skills as a leader and as a soldier. Custer didn't like Hickey's desire to get into a fight, but Custer figured that would be beaten out of him one firefight at a time. Custer thought it was better to let the kid work that out of himself.

"Hickey. We have twenty minutes to be on that chopper." Custer pointed to the waiting green taxi. "I'll brief everyone once we are in the air. Go get the team moving."

"You got it, chief," Hickey replied, sliding the cool linked ammo back into its green metal canister with bright yellow letters painted on the side. He slammed the top down and resealed it by clamping down the latch, locking it into place. He grabbed the handle on top and another twenty-pound canister of 7.62 mm ammo for his M-60 and humped them toward the other men, who were resting in the shade of a tent. Hickey ran through the tent entrance and announced himself.

"Boss says we have fifteen minutes to be on that chopper," Hickey noted, throwing his head over his shoulder to point at the waiting Huey. The rest of the men looked up.

Sergeant Dave Hargis, his long hair tied back in a ponytail in definite disregard of army regs, looked up from his Martin D-18 guitar. He was plunking away on an old Blind Lemon Jefferson blues tune. Hargis liked the old Texas blues sounds, as he hailed from Beaumont, Texas. The high humidity of that area seemed to make him immune to the constant heat of Vietnam. He was marked as strange by the others for actually enjoying the monsoon season. "Reminds me of home," he would comment in his Texas drawl.

"I thought we were walking in tonight," he said, carefully putting the guitar away. He grabbed his well-worn leather holster, which held his Model 29 Smith & Wesson .44 Magnum. If asked, Hargis would reply that the massive handgun was "just for plinkin' at cans."

"No idea," Hickey said. "Fifteen minutes." Then he was back out the door to find his web gear, backpack, M-60 light machine-gun, M-16, grenades, and knife. Unlike many of the older men, Hickey had no real problem with the M-16. Then again, the later model he used had many of the kinks worked out from the earlier ones. Or maybe he just had pulled a rare decent one from the line in the armory. Besides, it was almost a sidearm to him, as he favored the much more powerful M-60. If he was down to his M-16, he had burned through all of his M-60 ammo.

Hargis bent over and laced one of his jungle boots tight, then lifted his leg back and kicked Yoder, who lay napping in a hammock.

"Wake up, you wretched commie," Hargis commented. "Time for war."

"I heard. I heard," Sergeant Larry Yoder mumbled. "Man, I was dreaming the most beautiful dream when Hickey came in and woke me up."

"What were you dreaming about?" Hargis asked, grabbing his other bootlaces and tightening them down.

"Thailand, man," Yoder whispered in reverence. "Thailand."

Everyone in the tent smiled at the thought of R&R in that paradise. No bullets, cheap booze, and women—those beautiful Thai women.

"Well, sheet, man, you are in Veet-Noom." Hargis mimicked LBJ's famous mispronunciation of the country's name. "Nothing here but hot beer, cold rice, and Victor Charles shooting at your sorry ass."

"I like Charlie. I respect him. He can fight," Yoder responded, rolling sideways in the hammock. Yoder ran his hand over his short-cropped black hair. He was of average height and build, with brown eyes years away from the bifocals he would need in his forties.

"That's why you're a commie pig. Now get up!" With that Hargis kicked Yoder again, forcing him to drop out onto the dusty floor.

Hargis finished strapping on his Smith & Wesson, and before Yoder could respond, he had his backpack and webbing on, had grabbed his AK-47, and was out the door. Hargis rejected the M-16 or CAR-15 for the far better Hungarian-made AK-47. Its superior larger bore, muzzle velocity, and lack of jamming appealed to many U.S. soldiers. You could bury it in the mud, run over it with a tank, come back a month later, and it would still fire.

"When General Giap takes over, I am definitely reporting your ass," Yoder yelled, pointing an accusing finger at his retreating audience. Now fully awake, Yoder soon had his gear and was also out the door to the chopper.

Born in Gettysburg, Pennsylvania, Larry Yoder came from Amish stock. His grandfather had broken away from them to join the Mennonites. His father had further continued the new family tradition of change and become a Southern Baptist. This was certainly a more liberal religious path than Yoder's Amish forefathers had walked, but it was still a strict one, and full of faith.

Larry had rejected a religious deferment based on his seminary studies and had volunteered for the army with the intention of going to Vietnam. Always a Calvinist worker at heart, he had gravitated to the Special Forces and excelled. He was now in his second tour of duty. Yoder liked the M-16 for its light weight. Humping spare ammo through the bush was not his idea of fun; besides, their missions were usually designed to avoid firefights.

The two team members left had already gathered their gear and were out the door on Yoder's boot heels. They were the quietest members of the six-man team.

Silent around people and invisible in the jungle, Sergeant Jeff Winkler hailed from the Pine Barrens region of New Jersey. As kids, Winkler and his friends had spent far more time outside in those vast forests and fields than inside. His best friend, Tom Browne, was the son of an Apache Indian in the air force. When the two boys were seven, Tom's grandfather had left the reservation in Arizona to live with his son and his family. He was eighty-four when he arrived.

The old man was a master tracker/scout Apache who had been raised in the old ways. He could track a mouse across rock if he had to. The old man—called Grandfather by Winkler and Tom—slowly taught them the ways of nature. Not by openly teaching them but by making the boys learn for themselves the lessons Grandfather gave them. He teased them with only enough information to make them think and discover for themselves.

For ten years Grandfather led the two boys. By the time he was seventeen there was no animal Jeff Winkler could not track; no bush or tree he did not understand. Though both boys were skilled, neither could beat Grandfather. He often proved this by sneaking up on them as they were stalking and kicking them in the rear and running off laughing. Even in his nineties Grandfather was as spry as a fit man in his fifties and outwitted the boys again and again.

Jeff Winkler was drafted right out of high school, and he took the path of the Green Beret. Once in Vietnam, Winkler was by far the best trail man anyone in the army had ever seen. There was no trip wire or booby trap that could trick his senses. He was a master at resetting those traps for those who had placed them. By understanding how nature flowed around him, he knew when something in the area was friend, enemy, or animal. There had been more than one occasion when his silent warnings by hand signals had turned an enemy ambush into the enemy's own doom.

He carried a 5.56 mm Stoner rifle with the big 150-round plastic ammo box under it. He had traded with a U.S. Navy SEAL for this fine weapon. While his preferred weapon was a Gerber knife, which he could have out faster then the blink of an eye, for him there was nothing better than the Stoner for laying down lead.

Winkler's idea of R&R was going off into the jungle alone to study the exotic plants and animals of Vietnam. He regularly traveled into areas heavily owned by the enemy, but he always returned unscathed, and often with solid intel. His knowledge and eyes made the entire team glad to have his skills on their side.

The final member of the team to head toward the waiting helicopter was Sergeant Dan Hadad. Like Hargis, he was from Texas, but he had grown up in the large oil town of Houston. Having joined the ROTC in high school, he had known then that the military would be his first stop in life after graduation. Like so many his age, he was spurred on to do his duty in Vietnam by a father's or uncle's service in World War II.

With his family roots going back deep to the Russian-held Latvia, where his grandfather had escaped during the Russian Revolution, Hadad was a natural rebel against authority. With dark, wiry hair, he had surprising strength for his five-foot-ten, 175-pound frame. Hard as a rock, Hadad could climb ropes like a monkey, faster then anyone else around him, by using his arms alone. He was fearless in battle.

He had decided to ignore college until after the war and joined up straight out of high school. He had gone to Special Forces just to be with the best, and he had earned respect among his peers in two previous tours. Now on his third, he figured that he would go back to college now that the war was winding down.

Hadad favored the heavy M-14 rifle. With .30 caliber rounds, it had been the main army rifle until the M-16 had been introduced in 1964. The older Special Forces soldiers tried out the new weapon with its .223 mm round and found it lacking. It jammed, it was of limited use in firing over fifty feet into a jungle, and, worst of all, it did not stand up well to the brutal heat, killer humidity, and daily rains of Vietnam. Many of the Green Berets dumped the new M-16 and went back to their trusty M-14s. Hadad had also picked up that weapon when he came in-country in 1969. He also toted an M-79 "blooper" 40mm grenade launcher and various rounds for it.

One by one, the men loaded themselves into the waiting Huey. They secured their gear, facing each other from different sides of the chopper. As the pilot wound the engines up and the rotors built speed, Captain Fred Custer handed the orders to the man next to him, who would read them and then pass them on. There were no words about the mission, and none would be spoken until they were alone again as a team on the ground.

Custer liked security. He knew that a word overheard in camp or even by the pilot could find its way to the ears of the enemy. He had trained his men not to say anything about a mission unless they were sure that everyone around was known, trusted, and proven. The Huey pilots were unknown. They were just a taxi service to the firebase in the south, from which the mission would deploy. Custer's attitude had kept the team safe and brought them home for the night more then once.

As the rotor blades were coming up to takeoff speed, Mac came running from his command post. He ducked under the whirling blades and handed a piece of paper to Custer. Mac had to yell to be heard.

"Here's some 155 and 175 frequencies if you need them. They can cover you about halfway in. And the base Top knows where you will be. You can trust him to keep the news off of the front page and call him in a pinch. Good luck, Custer." With that, Mac was away from the chopper and watching as it rose. Fred Custer gave him a quick salute, which Mac returned.

As the chopper took off and began the journey south, each man read the orders from Saigon and absorbed their implications. Custer stared out over the jungle canopy as they flew through the air. He wondered what this mission would bring.

CHAPTER 2

Don't cut off too much of the map showing your recon zone
(RZ). Always designate at least 5–10 kilometers surrounding
your RZ as running room.

—POI 7658 Special Forces Combat Manual ROV 1970

CAMBODIA—JANUARY 1973

A T MIDNIGHT, LARRY YODER WAS LYING on his back, fingers intertwined behind his head, staring up at the bright stars through a hole in the upper jungle canopy. The soft loam of Cambodia absorbed his weight, and the fragrant night aroma filled his nose and mind.

He was thinking about Saint Paul and his letters to the early Christians. Larry wondered what Saint Paul would have written had he been in Vietnam. Probably the same things, Larry concluded as he closed his eyes. The rest of the men were spread out close by.

They had choppered in from Phuoc just after dusk. At the firebase, after organizing everything to his satisfaction, Custer went with his men and grabbed some chow. The food was made by locals and spicy hot, but that was fine. Better to smell like a local in the jungle than an American sweating out his C-rats. Charlie had a great nose.

As they sat eating and bullshitting, Custer ran the operation through his head again, trying to make sure he had everything planned right. He wondered if he had worked everything out well enough. Did he have all the maps, information, and materials they would need? He was glad that they weren't following the path the armchair warriors back in Saigon had picked for them.

After coming in from their firebase to this one just outside Duc An in Quang Duc Province, the first thing Custer had done was check in with the Special Forces Top there, an old soldier named Ray Beal. Beal had joined the Special Forces back in the fifties, long before Kennedy's speech and Barry Sadler's song had made the elite unit a household word. Most Green Berets hated the song.

Mac had already radioed Beal and told him the situation. Beal had no beef with Fred Custer and his men coming into his area. It was a crazy war, after all, but it was the only war they had right now.

Beal had gone over the orders and maps with Custer and assured him that the drop-off point was fine. Then Beal had dug out his personal maps of the area where Custer and his men were going. He handed these over.

"Whoever planned this has never seen the area on foot. They have you going straight into a swamp and humping through it for five klicks," Beal noted, pointing at the map. "If you want wet feet and a bunch of leeches, it's a great way to get them."

"What would you suggest?" Custer asked, wanting neither.

"Well, there's a little trail runs through here." Beal thumped his thick finger on the map. "It's marked. We like to parallel it when we go into that area. But we haven't been out that way in three months. They have you going in deep, brother."

Both men knew better than to walk on a known trail or path. It was much safer to parallel it to either side thirty yards out.

"The wheel's rigged, but hey, it's the only game in town," Custer mused.

"True," Beal agreed. "You take my map. I have other copies. The 155s and air cover know all the plots I have down on it. We finally got 'em trained. And that egress point, I wouldn't go anywhere near it. Our recent intel says that a division of NVA are parked there. General Giap's finest; tanks and all. No, head the opposite direction from there to here."

Again Beal thumped a thick finger down onto the map. "She's marked. We've used it before, and it's clean. As safe as you're going to find in bandit country."

"Thanks," Custer replied, sliding the map behind the clear plastic top of his canvas map holder.

They shook hands and headed for the mess hall. Custer's and Beal's men were already there, trading tales of Bragg, war stories, and adventures with five-dollar Saigon whores. After chow, the smokers grabbed a last cigarette, because there would be none in the field. They had been trained and learned from experience that anything that could give them away in the jungle in fact would give them away. It was dangerous enough work without advertising to the enemy.

The food and the hot Vietnamese sun both took their toll, so they rested in the shade, waiting for the sun to drop from the sky. They would chopper out at dusk. Two other Hueys would go ahead of them and land in different spots away from the real drop-off point. This was a trick learned from experience. The enemy would have three points to check out. Hopefully, Custer and his men would slip away safely, like shadows, undetected, into the jungle.

Had the enemy known which men were coming to pay them a visit that night, every enemy unit would have been alerted and out looking for them. Custer's men were known to the North Vietnamese and Viet Cong forces all the way to Hanoi. They were well known, respected, and despised.

Custer and his Montagnards were feared in their region for having thwarted or kept in check many NVA operations in the past year. Each American on his team had a reward of twenty-five thousand piastres on his head. Fred Custer had a fifty-thousand-piastre reward on his. That was about four thousand dollars American, and a fortune to the comrade who would never collect it.

The Special Forces team had even earned a nickname among the local enemy soldiers: "the night vipers." It was Winkler who ferreted out the information after hearing references to "night vipers" from a local villager. He had thought it would be a new animal to track and study, sketch, and add to his thick notebook of local flora and fauna. It had taken half an hour of his broken Vietnamese and the villager's broken English to get past the language barrier and discover that he was one of the night vipers.

The team all laughed and loved it. They had already collected a couple of the reward posters of themselves and hung them with pride in the team house, where cold Cokes, beer, and hot whiskey waited in between missions. The rewards meant that they were hurting the NVA, and their leaders in Hanoi knew it. The nickname, however, meant that they were respected in the jungle. It was a badge of honor. Captain Fred Custer made sure that they earned that badge.

In the world of Special Forces, Custer was a thorough planner and went beyond even the recommended training or usual standards. He didn't just check and double-check, he went deeper. Like a wasp building a nest, Custer had not only the instinct but the training and the tools to build a superior one. No one demanded more from his men than Fred Custer. No one pushed them harder. But these men liked being pushed that way, and they respected him. That came from Custer being tougher on himself than he was on any of his men.

Then the myth began.

In his first tour as a Special Forces team commander, Custer was with some of his men in a cheap Saigon dive drinking off some anger. They were drunk, they were loud, and they didn't care who was there. A West Point major, from a table in the corner, came over and confronted them. Greg Wiltshire, now rotated back to the land of milk and honey, laughed and pushed the man away.

Unknown to Custer's men, that West Point major was speaking for a one-star general at the table in the corner of that smoke-filled bar. What a general was doing in that place no one ever figured out. It was like seeing an albino dwarf shoot out from the sidelines of an NFL game to play quarterback. It made no sense.

But there he was, and soon that general was the one in Wiltshire's face, and he was not asking that the men quiet down. Generals do not ask. Wiltshire, too drunk to see or care about that single star on the man's shoulder, told him to fuck off. The general grabbed him by the lapel. Wiltshire leveled that general with one punch and turned away and went back to talking to the mama-san who owned the place.

The bar went silent.

When he was told later what he had done, Wiltshire had no recollection of the moment. It should have ended his career; gotten him a court-martial and assured him a long stay in Leavenworth. It was Fred Custer who worked his mojo magic and smoothed things over. He and the general went back to the table in the corner. Drinks were brought. There were heated words, but Custer did not back down. Somehow, he calmed the pending one-star storm and got Wiltshire off the hook. The respect from his peers grew.

It took the promise of three Russian Tokarev 9 mm pistols, a couple of captured AK-47s, and a stack of NVA combat flags to smooth things over. Mac later helped Custer by buying the flags from the local village seamstress. She made them for the Americans to sell when they went back to Saigon. With a few bullet holes and some dabs of chicken or pig's blood, these brought a high premium in the capital city, far away from the shooting. Soldiers of all ranks who had never seen a shot fired in anger bought them and couldn't wait to get back home and tell their John Wayne tales.

The AKs would be easy enough to come by, but not the Tokarevs. Those were really scarce and valuable, as they came only from ranking enemy officers. With the deal struck and the promise of the goods to be delivered within a week, Custer quickly moved the men out of the club, leaving the general to do whatever the hell he wanted.

The word spread. Not only of Wiltshire's heroic deed—who didn't want to hit a general?—but of Custer getting it handled. Even Mac was impressed. He didn't even make it hurt when he handed over the three Tokarevs. He knew that officers who would go all the way for their men were a rare breed and had to be taken care of.

Over time, something else began to spread through the small world of the Special Forces soldiers: All of Custer's men went home alive. The myth began to grow around him.

His men felt more confident going into the field with him in charge. He was like some magic talisman protecting them all by using some rare combination of luck and skill. Skill could be taught and learned. Luck was either with you or it was not. Custer could not stop the rumors that swirled around him, and the myth continued to grow.

When a man was wounded in the knee on a mission, separated from the rest of the team, Custer had called in every helicopter gunship in the area for protective fire. Then he had charged in, cut the pack from the wounded man's back, slung him over his shoulder, and carried the man out, away from certain death.

The myth blossomed. If you went out with Captain Fred Custer, you came back alive.

He never left a man in the field. Never.

Fred Custer did not believe in luck. His was the world of preparation, hard training, proper intel, equipment, and the right men. Luck was for losers who waited for it to roll around on the rigged roulette wheel. Fred Custer was not a gambler. So he prepared and worked harder than anyone around him. There was nothing he would not do for his men. Nothing.

He earned their respect again and again in the jungles and in the camps. Over time there was not a man who served with him who would not jump over the side of a mountain, not knowing what was over the edge, if Custer asked him to. If he asked it, there was a good reason for it.

So as Larry Yoder lay pondering Saint Paul under the moonlight, Custer, once again, was running the operation through his head. He was making sure he had done everything humanly possible to assure that they all would make it home alive again.

Did they have enough ammo? Everything they needed in their packs? Were the radio frequencies right? Would the deadly artillery rounds respond if needed? Did they have enough food? Were there enough claymores hooked up if the flares on the perimeter went off? How quickly could they make it to the pickup point? Would the chopper pilots accidentally head to the original planned site? These and other questions flew through Custer's head.

The biggest question mark in his mind was Anh Pham, the forty-five-year-old Vietnamese man who had been assigned to take them into Cambodia. Pham not only knew the area they were going into but had relatives there. It was why he had been chosen. Never having worked with him, Custer had no idea of the man's worth. After they had been dropped off in Cambodia, on the fifteen-klick hike through the jungles before they stopped, Pham had more than kept up with the Americans. Silently he followed, never missing a beat or slowing them down. He was OK in the jungle, the Green Berets thought.

Custer worried that the stranger would get them killed or, worse, had somehow gotten word of the mission back to the other side. So many of the Vietnamese wore a South Vietnamese Army uniform while their true sympathies lay with the North.

Had Custer known Pham better, he would not have worried at all. It was true that Anh Pham had once fought for the North, but that was long ago. Besides, Anh Pham was not political; his interest was survival.

Like so many of his countrymen, he loved Vietnam. It didn't matter to him if Saigon or Hanoi was in charge. Like yin and yang, both carried good and bad with them. Pham was like the wind; he was able to flow in and around the obstacles of politics. What general or president was in charge far away did not matter. What did matter was how the rice came in or how the water buffalo moved. It was his family that rose above all other concerns in his mind and deeds. Above all else, Anh Pham loved his family, and everything he did was done to keep them safe.

Born in North Vietnam in 1925, Anh Pham had joined the war against the Japanese in 1941. He had been in the camp of none other than Ho Chi Minh himself back then. When the Japanese were chased out, Ho begged the Americans for help against the French, only to be spurned. So, using U.S.-supplied World War II weapons and a trickle of newer Chinese guns, Ho took his war to the French, and Anh Pham followed.

He was captured, and his intelligence, natural language skills, and personality made him a valuable asset for the French soldiers far away from their homes. They liked Anh and used him to translate for them in the villages. Plus, he somehow made fine bottles of French wine appear when needed. This was no easy task in a war zone halfway across the world from Paris. So, again flowing like the wind, Pham became a supporter of the South.

Then one day, a hard veteran colonel of the French Foreign Legion who had once worn a German SS uniform saw the coming doom of his current army's efforts. He had seen doom before. He pulled Anh Pham aside and, in his German-accented French, informed him of reality. Since it was known that he had come from the North, Pham would be killed before the French pulled out if he did not become a member of the South Vietnamese Army. This was a minor shift in the wind, and so Pham joined the ARVN.

The beaten French left, and he moved to Saigon, where he rose in stature and rank. He married, and his first daughter, Ann Pham, was born. He had other children, who grew as the U.S. involvement grew. They lived in Saigon, went to good schools, and, except for trips to see their grandmother in the family village, were sheltered from the war.

Anh Pham, however, was not. He saw that the Americans would soon leave. After that South Vietnam would quickly fall. He was already making the needed plans, bribing the correct officials. Soon he and his family would escape Vietnam and find a new home in America. Once again the wind would flow around obstacles. This was good for survival, so this was good for his family.

Anh Pham would do anything for his family.

He packed only an old American Colt .45 on his hip. He did not expect to use it. With an unfired weapon it would be much easier, if they were captured, for Pham to shift the winds to his advantage. He could convince the North Vietnamese that he had been forced to come along, that he had no real convictions in favor of the Americans.

Fred Custer did not know all of this or he would not have worried. He also did not know about the tiger who padded silently close to them. Had Custer known about the silent tiger, he would have done something other than sit and run potential problems through his mind.

Mr. Pham felt the tiger in the night. Because he had spent a long time in the jungle, he knew of its power. He was unsure whether the tiger was a good omen or a bad one. As in all of life, time would tell.

Winkler felt the tiger also. He had tracked the magnificent cats in the jungle. Once he had even stalked one and touched its flank. The lightning-fast reflexes of the jungle animal were even quicker than he had expected. Winkler had the advantage since he was the hunter, and he quickly moved away and climbed a tree. The tiger roared and circled the tree, asserting its dominance. Winkler calmly waited.

Eventually, satisfied that he had prevailed, the tiger slipped away. For Winkler the feel of the thick orange-and-black-striped fur under his fingertips had been worth the risk.

Tonight, though, he felt a different tiger in the night. Like Anh Pham, he was not sure what this meant. Had he the time, he would have prayed and meditated, but this moment in this war was not the place for that.

War is an odd thing. It brings out the best in some men and the worst in others. Always the innocent suffer from the will of these clashing forces. No one ever knows what to expect; complete silence one moment and a living hell of flying metal and dying men the next.

War always tests the eternal questions of destiny, fate, and free will. These men were all there of their own free will, after all. The question was, were they destined to be there at that moment? Was it fate that unfolded the events of the next few moments, or was it bad luck? Was it bad planning, or were the stars out of alignment? Was the tiger sent to begin the chain of events that horrible night, or was it just a force of nature meeting technology in the jungle of a war?

Trip wires connected to flares had been set up around their camp. The intention was that if an enemy hit a wire, a warning would go up to Custer's men. The flares were far enough away that their exact location would not be revealed but close enough for them to react as needed.

When the tiger's front paw hit a wire, the animal quickly dropped back to examine this new experience, assessing it as a threat. What the tiger didn't expect and had never seen before was the blinding, white-hot phosphorous flare that shot up into the air. This flare shattered the calm of the night, turning thirty yards of the area into a bright white, overlit landscape for a moment. The tiger escaped into the night.

All the men were up instantly, fingers on triggers of weapons that came into the men's hands by instinct. Because of their training and experience, they quickly spread out, forming a circle around Anh Pham, weapons pointing outward. The threat might not come from the direction of the tripped flare.

Safeties on the weapons were quietly released; gleaming rounds of brass waited under cocked hammers ready to be let loose. The men were silent, ears also cocked. At night a sound would tell them far more than their eyes could.

When there was nothing but silence for a few moments, Winkler crept up beside Custer and whispered in his ear. In times like this, Custer was always caught off guard by the quiet tracker. The man could move beyond human silence when he wanted to. Winkler whispered to Custer that he would go check it out, and Custer nodded in agreement.

The others watched him move off into the jungle on the balls of his feet, one foot in front of the other until he was just a shadow melding with the jungle. His footsteps formed a single line instead of the left and right ones most men left. The men could hear nothing as he glided through the vines and limbs of the bush; the jungle parted for him as if it knew he was of it.

They all waited in anticipation until he returned a few moments later. "Tiger" was all he whispered to each man individually, his voice so quiet that only the person he spoke to heard what was said to him. They relaxed somewhat. Fingers came off of triggers. When he got to Anh Pham to whisper what had tripped the flare, he was surprised when the Vietnamese spoke first.

"Was it the tiger?" Mr. Pham asked in his quiet English.

"Yes," came the surprised response. "How did you know?"

Mr. Pham only smiled and nodded as an answer. Winkler was sure that the man had not heard any of his whispers to the others. Some of these Vietnamese should not be underestimated, he was reminded again.

Custer and his men settled back down for the night, hoping for a few hours' rest before they took off at dawn, but a chain of events the tiger had set in motion would prevent that rest. Others saw that flare light up the night—and the night belonged to the devil and the North Vietnamese Army.

Two young scouts of the North Vietnamese Army saw the flare. After shared questions, one of them ran off to report this to their platoon leader. When that man got the news, he sent a runner up to the brigade commander. Then word was given down to the battalion major, a black-souled man. He hated all Americans for the death of his wife and child in a B-52 bombing raid on his village.

The report fit the facts. Three helicopters had been sighted in the area. They had searched but found no traces of men. Now he knew where at least one group had ended up.

If there were Americans in his area, he would root them out and destroy them. If he was fortunate, one or two would be brought to him alive and his camp would fill with the sounds of their torture for hours. The major would send their souls away as lost ghosts to wander the jungle forever.

His orders went out, and the units began the hunt. The major calmly waited. He opened his wallet and stared by candlelight at his only fading photograph of his beloved wife and child. His rage once again rose. Yes, he hoped that at least one of the Americans would be taken alive.

Runners went out of the major's camp, and word went down the very disciplined battalion lines. The battalion was broken down into platoons that fanned out in a human arc, which began to advance on sandals made from U.S. tires or marched in Chinese combat boots. They moved out across the night. They wanted to find and uproot the invaders, to kill the hated Americans. Bolts were pulled back so that 7.62 mm rounds slid into the oiled chambers of their Chinese-supplied AK-47s. Every round fired was a step closer to their pending victory.

Other runners from the major went to the division headquarters, for where there is a battalion there is a division. This division towed along heavy Russian- and Chinese-made artillery. If he needed it, the major would break radio silence to bring that artillery to bear down upon the enemy.

It took an hour for the first NVA platoon to trip another one of the flares near Custer's camp. The shock of the white light caused a sixteen-year-old soldier to accidentally pull the trigger on his Soviet-made SKS rifle. His rounds shattered the calm night. His comrades, hearing shots, joined in firing their various weapons at unknown targets. The sixteen-year-old died in a crossfire from those bullets.

Custer and his men knew it was no tiger this time. They were quickly awake, weapons ready, watching the silhouetted figures under the falling flare. They held their fire.

Their mission was not to engage the enemy but to get to that POW camp and report back. So they moved out quickly and silently away from the threat in a classic figure-eight technique. The men moved like a well-oiled machine through the night. One of them stood with the muzzle of his weapon pointing back to where they had just been. When the last man was past him, he faded back and another held that covering position. Like some strange armored caterpillar, they flowed through the jungle.

Had they only encountered a small group of NVA, they would have gotten away, but they were up against a full battalion of men out hunting them. A battalion led by a black-hearted major who wanted their asses.

That arc of platoons moving out had already flanked Custer and his men.

Had they known this, the Special Forces team would have really cut and run. They would have dropped extra weight like food and packs and really done a didi, running away from the enemy lines to the safety of their pickup. Had they known that the NVA division was not in its last known position but had moved between the path they were on and the POW camp they were heading to, they would have fled in earnest.

Instead they landed right in between two more platoons who were out looking for them. Hickey ran smack into one of the soldiers. His hard 210 pounds hit the five-foot-four, hundred-pound, seventeen-year-old boy like a rock. The boy went down, and Hickey didn't hesitate. He dropped onto the soldier's chest, clamped a hand over his mouth, and sank his K-bar knife deep into his chest cavity, twisting his wrist hard. He felt the strangled cry and felt the boy's chest fall for a final time.

With his final breath leaving his body, the dying soldier pulled the trigger on his World War II vintage M-1 Garand, and a .30-06 round started the real firefight.

Other men from that boy's platoon opened up at nothing more than the noise of that rifle shot. Hot rounds flowed through the air, the red Chinese tracers filling the night like demonic fireflies.

Hargis returned the fire with his AK-47. Winkler opened up with the Stoner, and Yoder let his M-16 rounds fly. Custer threw grenades, and Hadad's blooper sang. Hickey opened up with his deadly M-60. These men knew where the enemy was located from the red tracer lines, and the team's return fire was devastating. They broke those two platoons and sent them running.

Nevertheless, other platoons had moved in from both sides, attracted by the noise. They opened up, and suddenly Custer and his men found themselves in a dangerous crossfire between two opposing forces. That was the last place you ever wanted to be. So they ran again, with the red tracer rounds chasing them into the night.

The North Vietnamese major was informed of what was going on. Smiling, almost hearing a live American screaming once again under his knife, he began to close the pincers of his army.

The running battle went on like this for half an hour, a deadly game of cat and mouse. The major lost men but didn't care about that. He could always get more men. He wanted the Americans—but they were not staying in place as most units under attack would. They kept moving, and soon he would lose them. They were slipping through his grasp, and that must not be allowed to happen. The major broke radio silence, and the NVA artillery was brought into the game.

With every round Custer and his men fired, they had less ammo to keep the fight going. Hickey had already burned through half of his M-60 ammo. The grenades were all gone now. There was no time to set up any of the remaining claymore mines with their hundreds of deadly double-ought steel balls, which could ravage any enemy line. No time. They were really running now.

After assessing the situation, the major studied the last known position of the Americans and plotted ahead of them in the path he thought they were running along. He called that position in to the big division guns. If Custer and his men had been running in a straight line, that might have killed them.

They didn't move in a straight line, though. No sane man would, and certainly no Special Forces men would. They had been using the zigzag escape technique as they ran. Move and change directions, move and change directions.

The heavy rounds began to rain down, ripping the ground open. The air screamed and the earth moaned from the hot shards of steel. The major's commands brought that rain of death down upon his own men, but he didn't care.

For whatever reason—fate or free will—the far edge of that artillery barrage came down where Captain Fred Custer and his men were. The night erupted with blossoms of yellow-red fire, and flying metal forged in hell danced around the Green Berets. The noise deafened them. The heat singed their hair as they all flattened to the ground.

One of them hadn't moved fast enough. A burning piece of hot metal ripped through Fred Custer's back and bored its way into his lower spine. One piece of metal weighing only two ounces would change his life forever.

The others saw him go down. They surrounded their leader and held tight. Their cold, precise fire cut down any enemy soldier foolish enough to approach and kept the rest at bay.

Now the heartless major ordered all of his troops onto the known position of the Americans. No more artillery. He wanted to taste their deaths. The NVA moved in and began to close the pincers of death again.

Yoder gave Custer first aid and checked for other wounds. He only found the pencil-wide hole where the shrapnel had gone in at the base of the spine. Hadad got on the radio and called for choppers to grab them at the rally point Beal had given to Custer. Custer had made sure every man on the team knew it by heart.

The radioman who received the message sent another soldier to wake up XO Ray Beal. Beal had told them personally to come get him if anything came up that night. He was like a mother hen watching a brood of chicks. These were now his men to cover for as long as they were in his area.

Beal acted fast. First he got the choppers into the air for a pickup. The pilots hesitated, as it was night, but Beal's look got them moving. No one wanted to be on the Top's shit list. Beal then called up the air force to see if they had anything up in the air. Then he woke up the mighty 155 mm howitzer batteries. These men were happy to respond, sensing decent targets to bring their batteries to bear upon after months of frustration.

Beal personally spoke to Hadad and got their exact map grid

position. He told him to get the team moving to the pickup point as fast as he could. Get moving and now! Then Beal got the artillery air liaison officer on the line and fed the 155s the plots on the grid.

The massive American guns let loose the horrors of war upon the enemy lines.

The men who thought they were closing in for a kill became the victims. First 155 mm smoke rounds slammed into the position. Hadad confirmed these as being on target before he took off, following the rest of the team. The main force of the NVA division was parked well out of range of the deadly American guns, but now, chasing the A-Team, the soldiers of the NVA battalion had moved in too close. They were within range. Their major, in his rage, had erred.

"Fire for effect," the ALO calmly ordered his gunners. "Fire at will. Give 'em all you have."

So the near-hundred-pound rounds flew through the air to stop the advancing lines of the NVA battalion. They were caught in the open with nowhere to run. Private Marcos Sanchez slammed the fat, cold brass of a 155 mm round into the breech of the gun, and Private David Powell let that first round fly into the night.

The U.S. gunners walked hundreds of the projectiles up and down and left and right of the friendly position: WPs, HEs, and Firecrackers, each of those letting loose sixty antipersonnel bombs to dance among the NVA, to cut the enemy down. It was a massive and horrible barrage, leaving little untouched.

A squadron of F-105s returning from an aborted mission, loaded with wing canisters of unused napalm, were called onto the target by Beal. The flyboys were more than happy to oblige, not wanting to return to their base still loaded with unused ordnance. It took them all of five minutes to get from where they were over Vietnam into a bombing formation to cover Custer and his men's retreat.

Hickey threw Custer over his broad shoulder and turned to run as the rest of the team moved away from the coming death. They ran without regard for themselves. They ran for Captain Fred Custer's life.

The jellied napalm rolled across the ground and ignited, trapping the NVA who remained. It flowed over them like an ocean wave, opening up into a web of sticky fire that could bore a hole through to a man's bones. It corrupted all it touched in a baptism of flaming hell. Those touched by it screamed and burned. If they were lucky they died.

Custer's men felt that terrible heat chasing them as they ran. They cut packs and ran like they had never run before.

They ran for their captain.

RECENT DAYS

CHAPTER 3

If you show confidence, your team will have confidence.

—POI 7658 Special Forces Combat Manual ROV 1970

VERO BEACH, FLORIDA—JUNE, LAST YEAR

MAJOR TED HICKMAN, RETIRED TWO YEARS now, stepped out of the Learjet and took the five short steps down onto the hard concrete runway of the private Vero Beach airport. He was not used to the luxury of the small chartered jet that had delivered him across the nation. Hickey was much more accustomed to the beastly air force C-5As or, in the final decade of his military career, the commercial airliners the army had the soldiers use. After experiencing the clusterfuck the civilian airlines had become post-9/11, he preferred a C-5A ride when he could grab one.

Even with the uncomfortable canvas webbing seats and rough ride, and usually surrounded by military equipment, not only did he feel at home in a military plane, but he didn't have to deal with the slow-moving, winding lines and ever growing security checks. While Hickey understood security, as far as he could tell, the civilian system lacked it. Any Vietnamese sapper could have penetrated it.

The Florida heat rose from the baked concrete and sucked the air from his lungs. It was hot. Not Iraq hot, but hot enough. He hefted his one well-used green duffle bag over his shoulder and headed for the shade of the small airport terminal. A car and driver were supposed to be waiting for him.

As he approached the small building, he saw a dark-suited young man, wearing two-hundred-dollar Ray-Ban sunglasses, standing by the entrance. The man held a sign with clean, large block letters reading HICKEY. Hickey paused and looked around. He was not expecting a suited chauffeur. A driver, to him, was a private with a Humvee.

Hickey walked up to the young man. "I'm Hickey," he said.

"Major Ted Hickman?" the driver asked, slipping a photo of Hickey back into the coat pocket of his custom-fitted thousand-dollar Armani suit. Even in the heat, the man didn't break a sweat.

"Major Ted Hickman, retired."

"Please, sir, who sent for you?" the driver asked, immobile.

"Colonel Fred Custer, retired," Hickey replied. So Custer still ran a tight ship, security and all. Hickey didn't know where Custer had acquired the photo the driver had, but he figured that the old hound still had a few contacts back in D.C.

"May I take your bag, please, sir?" the driver asked, holding out his arm.

The way the words flowed, they became a statement, not a question. Hickey was definitely not used to a man carrying his bag around, but then he was in the civilian world now. He took the bag down from his shoulder and let the chauffeur take it.

"Are there any more pieces of luggage, sir?" the young man asked.

Luggage? Luggage was what people going to Paris jammed their clothes into. Hard leather or plastic cases with SAMSONITE on little silver labels attached to them. Never in his life had Ted Hickman heard a military canvas duffle bag called luggage.

"Just the one bag," he said, almost laughing.

"This way then, sir." The driver smartly turned and led the way through the small airport terminal. Hickey followed like a stranger in a foreign land learning the local customs, which in many ways he was.

This was a new world for him. For over thirty years, his life had been in the military. His only friends had dressed in combat green or formal dress uniforms, where everyone read your fruit salad like a résumé. After Vietnam, Hickey had stayed on in the army. He liked his place within it, and the army had rewarded him over the years with new challenges, adventures, and rare battles. Even at fifty, the street fighter had never been beaten out of him. Hickey still loved a good fight.

The Army had given him a few wars and let him see the world as not many ever do. He had stayed on in Vietnam through the fall of Saigon in 1975, when he had choppered out with the last lucky ones as that drama's curtain closed.

He had seen the harsh deserts of Iraq and Saudi Arabia, and the more civilized Japan, Thailand, England, Germany, and France. Hickey had walked the jungles and humped the mountains of Central and South America. The frozen ice of Greenland had tested his will to live, and the high, desolate mountains of Kipling's grim stepmother had almost cost him his life. A Russian Hind helicopter had caught him and the rebels he was with exposed. Only a lucky shot with a Stinger by an Afghan kid had saved their hides that time.

Hickey could easily have worked his way up from Fort Bragg into the confusing maze of the Pentagon. With his contacts and his 201 file, he could have gone anywhere in the army that he wished.

Although sitting behind a desk was not where the action was. You became old and out of shape. Even at fifty, Hickey could outrun most men in their thirties.

So he had steered clear of advancement and a doomed desk jockey position to remain in the Green Berets. He knew that there he could rise only so far in rank, but to Hickey, the rank of major was fine. He would have enjoyed being a sergeant major for a good battalion or division officer, but that would have meant leaving the Green Berets. So Hickey stayed and immersed himself into his beloved Special Forces as an Olympic swimmer would dive daily into the water working toward a gold medal.

He also stayed away from the other path more than open to a man with his talents. In the closing days of Vietnam, Hickey had seen and felt the black ops presence. It was a tempting, murky world one could easily slide into. No rules. Unlimited funding. That black curtain could envelop one in a cloak of protection that few could penetrate. You could disappear if you wanted. But that all came with a price, and Hickey the street fighter, the survivor, did not like the costs he saw. After escaping the darkness of the tough New York streets, he found that he much preferred the light.

Used to a rough Humvee ride, Hickey had never been in a limo. The driver slipped the duffle bag into the trunk, then walked around and opened the back door to the classic Lincoln. It was jet black, and the chauffeur's suit matched it. Hickey looked up at the emotionless face of the driver before stepping in and letting the thick leather seat absorb his weight.

The driver looked down and pointed. "You'll find a small refrigerator with refreshments, sir. And the telephone is over there." He pointed to another section of the expensive automobile. "And there is a full bar, of course, sir."

"Of course," Hickey wryly commented.

The limo door closed, sealing him in a cold, air-conditioned environment. The heavy tinting of the glass shielded the occupants from the brutal Florida sun. More out of curiosity than out of feeling the need for anything, Hickey explored the lavish custom Lincoln. The bar was well stocked, and there was even ice and a little sink. Turning a knob, he was surprised that water flowed from it. Hickey thought this unnecessary as he shut it off and opened the refrigerator.

He had seen ones like it in hotels, but they did not stock the expensive waters, caviar, olives, cheeses, beers, and champagne this one did. Hickey settled for a bottle of water. As he twisted the top off, he took one more look at the contents of the refrigerator. He didn't know wines or caviar, but he figured that these were among the best available. He kicked the door closed and drank his water.

Fred Custer had sent for him, and Custer could afford the best these days. Hickey was not sure why Custer had called, but that didn't matter. It was his captain from Vietnam who called him away from his new Arizona home. Hickey had responded without question, boarding the private jet to Florida. If Custer called, it must be important, Hickey thought.

After that small piece of shrapnel had cut into Fred Custer's spine on that terrible night, he had lost consciousness. He had slipped away from the moment via the morphine injections Yoder had slammed into his thigh, floating into a painless sleep.

The following weeks had been a blur of drugs, hospital beds, and murmuring voices of which Fred Custer recalled little. He had been flown out of Cambodia back to the firebase in South Vietnam from which they had originally staged.

From there he had been choppered into Pleiku, to the 71st Evac field hospital of II Corps. A good Red Cross nurse named Marcy Troy had stabilized him. Then a good doctor named Rob Renzler had examined the serious wound that had cut Custer's spine and had known that his patient would be better off in Japan. This VIP treatment had been assured by Mac, and Custer had been flown to Nippon.

Mac had been alerted to the injury within moments of the

Huey lifting the team out of Cambodia. Like a guardian angel, he had called in old debts all along the line, ensuring that his man was taken care of. Even a two-star general in Saigon had been awakened and reminded of a deadly night very long ago in Korea: Fred Custer was covered.

Custer had been sent to a fine young Army surgeon named Mike Cutforth. Long before Cutforth would open his exclusive private practice in Baltimore, he had served out his army draft in Japan operating on the maimed soldiers from Vietnam. That two-star general's weight had carried across the distance between the two countries, and Fred Custer had been taken care of.

Three nurses were assigned the task of checking over Custer's vitals twenty-four hours a day during their shifts. Anne Hellman watched over Custer from 7:00 A.M. to 3:00 P.M., when Christine Jeager would take over into the night; and from 11:00 P.M., like a mother hen watching her chicks, Peggy Wynne kept vigil until dawn. All three were good at what they did, and Fred Custer was prepared for the coming operation.

Dr. Cutforth did what he could. He first removed the two-ounce piece of twisted steel from the spine and dropped it with a clink onto a sterile stainless-steel tray. Just removing the metal was beyond the scope of many surgeons' abilities, but Cutforth's skillful, calm, slender fingers were more than up to the task. Then he examined the damage and knew that repairing it was beyond known medical science. He sewed his patient back up.

After Custer recovered from surgery, Cutforth broke the news to the young captain. Being the bearer of the news that a man would never walk again was never easy. Cutforth carried away a heavier burden each time he gave such news to a soldier.

Fred Custer was drugged, but not so deeply that he could not understand or respond to what was said to him. One never knew how a man would react to such life-altering words. Some cried. Some yelled. Others tried to rise out of their beds, breaking fresh sutures and reopening wounds. Some became silent, falling into a deep depression or a place few had ever been. Some even slowly willed themselves to die.

Nurse Hellman was at hand with a massive sedative if the doctor called for it. Neither had ever seen the reaction Fred Custer presented. Pensive, he was silent for two full minutes after hearing the doctor's pronouncements.

"Are you a good doctor?" he finally asked.

"They tell me I'm the best in the Pacific," Cutforth said, with no ego attached.

"Did you do all that you could?"

"Yes," came the quiet reply. "That and then some. I even had the newest journals on spinal injuries flown over to me from the States to see if there was some new technique. There isn't. Yours is a classic textbook example of a spinal cord injury. There is nothing more any doctor can do to repair the damage there."

"How long have I been out?" Fred queried.

"Three weeks."

"My men? Any of them . . ." The words trailed off at the thought of losing one of his men, being responsible when he might have been more prepared, or when he might have done something else.

"You were the only one hit," Cutforth replied. "They are all OK."

Custer fell silent for a long minute. The tick of the wall clock was the only sound in the room. Nurse Hellman waited with her fingers on the cool glass of the hypo full of sedative.

"What's my next step, Doc?" Custer asked, his voice rising. With that came Fred Custer's acceptance of his new life.

He faced months of rehab back in the States under a tough nurse named Ellen Williams. She refused to take no for an answer as she pushed the recovering soldiers in order to heal them. She was as tough as any DI Custer had ever met.

Well, Custer had been pushed before, and that didn't bother

him. He threw himself into the task of recovery, rebuilding his broken flesh, getting used to the wheelchair. He pushed his body, and—more important—his mind to accept the new position of rolling around in a steel-wheeled home. He wasn't happy, but he accepted the scars. He made a companion of the pain—not a friend, but something that just had to be accepted.

When he had repaired his body and mind as well as a human being could, he took to the offensive again. Ever the soldier, he made the army his latest opponent. The early word was for him to retire. They didn't have much use for wheelchaired troopers.

It took everything he could muster to remain in the army. He wasn't ready to leave her yet. Strings were pulled and old chits called in and friendships used. After all, the world of Special Forces is a small one. The men tend to know each other and each other's records. Word of a good or bad soldier was usually circulated well before the man would reach his new posting.

Custer was a very good soldier, and even those who didn't know him wanted to help him after reading his 201 file. Regs were bent. Corners were cut. Paperwork appeared and disappeared as needed. A position in the Pentagon was found. Custer was not perhaps the best qualified for it, but he would be at least competent until he learned the job fully.

So on a bright, sunny day in May of 1975, Captain Fred Custer rolled his new wheelchair into the Pentagon entrance and began his new life as a desk warrior. For a field man, one who enjoyed the feel of camo paint on his face and liked working with the Montagnards in their villages, it was a major adjustment. Custer, as he had always done, threw himself completely into the task and excelled beyond expectations.

Washington, D.C., became his new home. From that classified perch he could track the careers of the men with whom he had served. He was even able to help a few times when things got too hairy. He stayed in touch with the men, and they were all glad to hear from their former leader. Everyone would come visit him when in the D.C. area.

He slowly rose in rank until he reached colonel. Everyone around him knew he should have gone all the way to general and the Joint Chiefs of Staff. Two things prevented that. First, he was connected to that metal chair, and second, he was not a member of the West Point officers' club. Still, more than one general carried the results of Fred Custer's labors into a briefing for the president or the Joint Chiefs.

He also fell in love and married. Her name was Geraldine, and her petite body hardly gave the impression of the iron will and the sharp mind behind her soft brown eyes. They had met at an ambassador's party, and both felt the mutual attraction. She didn't mind the wheelchair, and she discovered her love of him. He fell completely for her. They were married in 1982.

In 1992, after a thirty-year military career, Fred Custer retired a full colonel. Even after they left the military, Custer and his troops remained friends. Custer always made sure he knew where he could find them, and he stayed in touch.

He and his pretty wife retired back to her native Florida, but he felt he was too young to quit working yet. Once he and Geraldine had settled in their Vero Beach home, Fred began to look around for something to do with himself.

Through his insider knowledge of the military- and government-funded ARPANET, which would soon explode as the Internet, Fred saw the potential of investing there. He immersed himself into the project and rooted around through technical journals and on the early bulletin boards until he saw what was coming.

Using funds saved just for such purposes, Custer invested early in the core companies that would build and maintain the infrastructure of the growing electronic network. From his military service, he knew which firms had the large contracts and would actually deliver the needed hardware and software. He lessened the danger of the high risk by spreading the investments across the board. He and Geri, as he called his loving wife, invested their risk capital and watched it grow beyond expectations.

They used that windfall to buy heavily into a young Internet company that rose near the sudden explosion of Northern California's Silicon Valley. It was Geri's search on the bulletin boards for an impossible-to-find toy that made them rich. She was looking for a birthday present for her young niece, a collector of Pez dispensers, which took them to the opening days of eBay. The search for that hunk of plastic led them to take half of their earnings and invest in the growing little company.

Although they weren't in on the ground floor, they were in early enough to watch their risk explode into a bank account in the millions before the nineties were finished. Once again Fred's luck and hard work had delivered. They used some of the money to build a beautiful beachfront home between the Indian River and the Atlantic Ocean. While it wasn't a mansion, it was no shack. From their patio they could smell the ocean air and watch in awe as the storms rolled across the Atlantic.

During all of those years, Custer had never forgotten his men. He had kept tabs on all of them, and when a situation had arisen that needed attention, he had made a call to Hickey in Arizona.

Custer had been surprised that Hickey didn't ask why he wanted to see him in person. Hickey had told him that he would be there as soon as he could book a flight. Custer told him not to bother, that he would hire a jet for him. Hickey had heard about the investments and knew the colonel was well-off financially. No one knew how well-off, but Hickey didn't object to the offer.

Orders were orders to old military dogs.

The limo cruised down Highway 1 toward the center of Vero Beach. The driver steered the car out onto 60 East and toward the ocean. Hickey stared out the windows at the mixture of new strip malls with their corporate stores and the older, established neighborhoods and shops.

Sitting happily upon the Atlantic Ocean, Vero Beach was halfway between Palm Beach and the Kennedy Space Center. It was a calm oasis away from the busy throngs that began at Palm Beach and grew southward, climaxing at the party zone at South Beach in Miami. Orlando was reachable, if need be, for the visiting relatives, but far enough away that it didn't impact Vero Beach much at all.

Only the annual snowbirds disturbed the idyllic setting. The natives were happy to see those escaping the winters up north come in for a few months and leave their money, but they were happier when the snowbirds went back home again in the spring. Then, until the next fall, they could kick off their shoes, relax, and be themselves. Not that they changed much during the winter season, but they could fully relax with the guests all back home.

Hickey didn't know any of this. All he saw was a quiet town with everything one would need to slide by. He had seen worse places in the world, but he wasn't sure he had seen better ones, at least not with his attitude those days.

Arriving back in the United States in retirement, after being so long overseas, he experienced culture-shock. Everything had changed so much. The America of 1971 he had left for Vietnam had certainly changed a lot. During his last decade of service, Hickey had been stationed overseas almost the whole time. Everything had changed on him while he had been away.

The mom-and-pop shops were being replaced by corporate establishments that made everything the same no matter where one went. This made the regional differences in the country slowly fade away, or at least take a backseat to the uniform corporate culture. While that influence seemed to be everywhere, there were still pockets of resistance. Vero Beach was one of those. No wonder Custer had landed here. It was a perfect place to call home for a man who had worn a uniform so long but always maintained a rebel streak within himself.

Hickey had chosen the open spaces of Arizona thirty miles outside of Tucson for his hideaway in retirement. He could easily get by on his retirement pay in the small ranch house surrounded by the large piece of land he had purchased. He woke each morning at 6:00 A.M., put on his running shoes, and jogged the desert for five miles, often stirring up the quiet animals of the sand. Staying in shape had long been drilled into him.

The big spread he had bought allowed him to keep his shooting skills up. The noise of the .30-06, 9 mm, and .45 rounds he fired didn't carry to any neighbors. He reloaded his own brass in the garage at night.

The sound of the driver speaking into a cell phone brought him back to the moment.

"I am approaching your driveway, sir," the driver said—to Custer, Hickey assumed. With that the driver snapped the cover closed on the cell phone and set it aside.

Hickey stared through the front windshield as the car rolled up a long road that led to a large light blue stucco house with Italian red tiles covering the roof. Hickey was happy to see the colonel rolling out of the front door to meet his guest. Hickey didn't wait for the chauffeur to open the door for him. He was up from the leather cushions and out of the limo before it came to a complete stop. While the driver was opening the trunk and getting the duffle bag, Hickey and Custer were shaking hands and smiling.

They exchanged sincere greetings after such a long time apart. They had not seen each other since Hickey had come through D.C. in the late eighties before deploying to England to cross-train with some SAS soldiers.

"Colonel, how the hell are you?" Hickey asked, smiling.

"Better now that you're here, Ted," came the warm reply.

Geri and the driver slid around each other at the car door. She quickly greeted Hickey before running back inside to lead the chauffeur through the house to deposit their guest's bag in his bedroom. Had Hickey known that the limo and driver had had to be called in from Orlando, he would have been even more impressed than he was. Vero Beach generally had little use for a limo service.

"Come on," Custer ordered, "let's go find a beer." He spun the wheels on his wheelchair and led the way. Custer refused to go the route of an electric wheelchair. By using a manual one he stayed in shape.

Hickey followed, closing the front door and letting the air-conditioning wrap itself around him again. He followed the colonel down a custom-built ramp into the living room and across the Persian rugs into the kitchen.

"You still drink beer, I hope, Ted. Retirement hasn't made an old man out of you yet, has it?"

"I still manage one or two. Sometimes even something stronger," Hickey shot back.

"Take your pick and we'll head to the patio. Good breeze today," Custer said, opening the door on his oversized refrigerator. He grabbed a bottle of Victoria's Brew from Victoria, Australia, a very rare find in the United States. Most of America seemed to think Foster's was the only beer or ale brewed in the land down under. Custer rolled his chair back out of the way so Hickey could grab his choice.

Hickey stared in wonder—the refrigerator was filled only with various beers, ales, and wines from around the world.

"Don't you people eat?" he asked.

"That"—Custer pointed across the vast kitchen to another oversized commercial refrigerator—"is for food."

Hickey grabbed a VB to try it and closed the door. With the colonel leading, he followed onto the patio.

The covered wooden deck was as oversized as the beer-filled refrigerator. Hickey had lived in military houses with less square footage.

On the deck, only the white beach was between the house and the lapping waves. The air smelled salty and clean. A long, sloped wooden ramp led down to the beach. Staring left and right, Hickey could see that the next houses were a long football field away on each side.

"Nice place" was all he could think to say.

"I've done OK for a cripple," Custer replied. "Sit down."

Hickey parked himself in a padded deck chair facing the ocean, and Custer wheeled up next to him, patting him on the shoulder.

"Damn, it's good to see you, Ted. It's been too long."

"Good to see you and Geri, Fred," Hickey replied.

They caught up on old times. Geri came out and joined them, her small body resting on Custer's lap in the wheelchair. Ted could see the attraction between them. She was a beautiful woman—five foot four, thin, with short dark hair and deep brown eyes from her Italian heritage. When she smiled, the day just got better. Hickey had only met her briefly before. He was looking forward to knowing her better.

She brought beer when the supply ran low; all three watched the daylight fade away as dusk set in. The first stars appeared, drilling holes in the night sky.

"So, why am I here, Fred?" Hickey finally asked, after Geri had slipped inside the house again.

"There's time for that later," Custer replied. "Let's go get some chow. There's a nice little place here in town that serves a mean crab."

"Sounds good. Lead the way, sir," Hickey said, setting the empty beer bottle down and waiting to be led once again by his first commander.

All three left the quiet beach and headed out in the Custer family Jeep Wrangler. They ate at a small restaurant that few knew about. Those who did tried to keep it that way.

CHAPTER 4

If the team leader loses his temper it will affect his judgment.
Keep cool and think ahead, always keeping an alternate plan
in mind. Don't be afraid to take advice from a team member.

—POI 7658 Special Forces Combat Manual ROV 1970

AFTER DINNER, THE NIGHT HAD LASTED long. They had returned to the beachfront home, and more beers had been dragged out, the empties joining their already fallen comrades. Custer had then brought forth a bottle of good whiskey, and he and Hickey had gotten down to some serious remembering.

The liquor had made some things easier to discuss, and they talked to each other openly about the lost years. They did not get drunk, but they got loose. Hickey listened; Custer talked, fingering a necklace with a ragged two-ounce hunk of steel on the end of it. Hickey figured out that when Custer was ready, he would tell him why he had called him; in the meantime, the two friends caught up under the moonlit breezes of the Atlantic coast.

Hickey didn't remember exactly when he went to bed, but his internal clock, long set by military rhythms, woke him at 6:00 A.M. Never one to miss his daily exercise—Hickey had once run his miles in a raging storm in the Philippines—he set off to find the beach. He was running on the beach by 6:05 A.M., putting in his five miles as the sun broke above the horizon.

The sand felt good under his feet as he whispered long-ago cadences to set a beat. He decided to push himself that morning to sweat the whiskey and beer from his blood. He increased the tempo.

After his run, where the sand met the waves behind the Custers' house, he kicked off his shoes, pulled off the T-shirt, and plunged into the cool ocean, the saltwater licking his flesh. After that he returned to the porch to let the sticky saltwater dry on his skin.

By the time he went in and took a shower and dressed, in shorts and a Florida imitation of a Hawaiian shirt, breakfast was being served. They ate scrambled eggs and sausage washed down with black coffee and orange juice before Hickey and Custer headed off to the docks. Fred had set up a deep-sea fishing trip for the day.

John Sterling ran a good charter service out of the Vero Beach docks. His boat, the *Grey Havens*, had been named after a place in his daughter's favorite book. It was well stocked and ready to go when Custer and Hickey drove up. Normally, Sterling took this time of the year off, but Fred Custer was a special customer. He had helped Sterling out of a serious jam one time and saved his boat from foreclosure. They were heading out into the ocean by 8:00 A.M. and had their lines wet by nine.

After the mate—an L.A. kid named Mike Slack, in Florida for the summer—dropped the lines into the blue waters, he faded away into the background. Sterling steered the boat, seeking some action while Custer and Hickey were left alone to wait for a fish to bite their bait. Custer broke the long silence and revealed why he had called Hickey on the telephone.

"You remember Yoder?" he began.

"Of course," Hickey replied. "One of Chairman Mao's secret instigators, as I recall." The old Special Forces camp joke brought a smile to both men's lips.

"Yes, him." There was more silence before Custer went on. "Well, after Vietnam, he quit dealing with Peking and went back to the seminary. He finished two degrees in divinity. Worked for the national headquarters of the Southern Baptist Church until the conservative reform of the early eighties. By the end of the decade, he was forced out."

Hickey just listened.

"He could have found other work, but he enjoyed spreading the word of God. He said it was his calling. So he started looking around for a small church from which he could sow the mustard seeds."

Both men sat in silence for a few moments as Custer gathered his thoughts. The reels ticked as the line played out, pulled by the movement of the boat cutting through the waves.

"He ended up here in Florida near the end of the nineties. Belle Glade." Custer turned and looked to Hickey. "There's a hell of a lot better places to end up than Belle Glade, Florida, Ted."

Custer pulled out a small leather cigar case and offered a cigar to Hickey. They each used a scaling knife to chop the ends off; Custer got his lit, then handed the old, beat-up 82nd Airborne Zippo over to Hickey. The distinct smell of lighter fluid filled the air as he, too, lit up. Both men sat puffing the fine cigars before Custer continued.

"It's like going to the third world down there. The local cops won't go into some places at night." Custer built the smoke up in his mouth and let it loose, the old dragon testing his breath again.

"Jamaican and Haitian immigrants living in tin shanties down on the lake or packed like sardines, twenty to a house or apartment. It can be a rough place. I tried to get him a better parish, but he wouldn't hear of it. He had found home. 'My flock needs me,' he used to tell me."

Hickey noted the past tense, and he didn't like it.

"Is he dead?" Hickey finally asked.

"I don't know," Custer said quickly, as he awakened from the memories of many long nights spent with Yoder. "He used to come up for dinner, or Geri and I went down there. Once a month for years. There's been no word for three months now."

A gull screamed, then dove into the water.

"That's why you're here, Ted. He and I had a system for communicating. After he started telling me about some trouble the local owners were giving him, we set up code words he could use on the phone or on the Internet. The last message I got from him was an e-mail, 'I'm praying to stop the coming hurricane.'"

"What did that mean?" Hickey asked.

"I think it meant that he was going to confront the head of the family that was giving him trouble. Hurricane meant trouble."

They paused and smoked some more.

"What kind of trouble, Fred?"

"Kid stuff at first. Slashed tires. Painted warnings on his car. But then it started getting worse. Words painted on the church door; warnings to the churchgoers to stay away. He came in one Sunday morning and found a gutted chicken on his pulpit. The blood covered his Bible. A Santeria warning, as best as we could figure out."

"What was he doing?" Hickey asked.

"He was trying to help those poor people who work the fields. He was trying to keep their kids in school and get medical care to those who needed it. But he also preached that Sunday was the Lord's day and not for work. Apparently he was succeeding there. The cane field owners down there run a 24/7 operation,

Ted. To them God is for those who can afford a good suit to go to church in."

More ticks from the reels.

"I called the local police. No help there. I later found out they are on the payroll for the cane company first. I hired the best private detectives out of Miami. They sent a man named Marshall Presnick. He's good, but also knows when to cut his bait and run. He spent a night in the local jail just for asking questions. His boss called me and returned my money."

"So what do you want me to do, Fred?"

"I need you to go down there. I need someone I can trust, someone Larry can trust. Someone who can handle himself and won't be scared away. No heroics. No John Wayne. I want you to do a recon for me. I need to know if Yoder is alive or dead."

Custer snapped his cigar overboard into the waves.

"If he's dead, I want the body, Ted. I want to bury him right. I need you to go find out. I'll do the negotiations, if need be, but I need to know who to talk to. Just go find out. I'd do it myself, but . . ." He slapped his useless legs.

"You never left a man in the field, Colonel," Hickey noted.

"And I'm not starting now."

It was a hard tone Hickey had not heard in a long time. They sat in silence.

"I'm your man," Hickey finally said—not that there was ever any doubt.

"Good, Ted. Good. I need you on this one. I need the street fighter," Custer said.

They lapsed again into silence.

"Why aren't these fish biting?" Custer broke the moment.

"Well," Hickey mused, "it would help if that mate had baited the hooks."

"You noticed that." Custer laughed.

"Yeah. I noticed."

"Well, I'm paying, and I wanted a few minutes to brief you." Custer turned to the wheelhouse.

"John, you have any bait on this barge?"

"Coming up," Sterling said, cutting the wheel and bringing the motors down to an idle. The L.A. kid reeled the lines in and baited the hooks.

CHAPTER 5

Do not retrieve your first expended magazine during contact,
because it will consume valuable time.

—POI 7658 Special Forces Combat Manual ROV 1970

WHEN LARRY YODER LEFT THE ARMY in 1974, like many with their insides scarred by the Vietnam War, he had sought out God for answers. As so many had discovered through the ages, he, too, found that the search raised more questions than it answered. He found, though, that his seminary studies were as good a place as any to bury the memories of the war and move on.

He had packed his army uniform away and walked back through the doors of the seminary to continue where his studies had been interrupted. He had finished his first degree in divinity and, still thinking the answers might be found within books alone, continued those studies. He had also been ordained.

After a second degree, Larry had come to the conclusion that he had better head out into the world again and away from the cloistered halls of academia. It was time to find his truths on the streets and to better serve God in His churches.

Yoder's instructors had noted the quiet young scholar and his ability to rise above the material presented. Yoder returned detailed examinations and explorations of the subject materials. Even religious studies fall within the rules of academia, and superior students are noted by the wise.

Those wise men had sent word around among their peers via the slow-moving letters of the day. Was there a place for such a bright young man with strong religious beliefs and a military record? Yes, there was. Yoder was wooed and stroked by the national headquarters of the Southern Baptist Church. They had a special need for a man who not only had deep religious beliefs and a will to carry forth the Word but also had military experience in far-off lands.

Yoder was hired and given the task of traveling the world to communicate in person with other churches in the cause, helping the Southern Baptist Church as he could. He was sent to Belgium, where he learned their form of French while eating peasant foods and drinking their plain wines, with which he was more than content. He traveled across Europe and even into the Soviet Union long before the official change of that country's politics away from hardcore Communism.

The GRU—the Glavnoye Razvedovatel'noye Upravlenie, Russian military intelligence—had a file on him. They had a file on every known U.S. Special Forces soldier. Besides, in those days every tourist inside the Bear's territory was followed as a matter of routine. Yoder was, of course, suspected of being with the CIA or some other U.S. intelligence agency. He was given special treatment by his hosts.

Coded messages were sent to the Russian embassy in Washington, D.C., to send word out to the Russian field agents in

America. They were to poke and prod where they could and check deeper into the background of the young Baptist who was visiting their country.

The Russians were very good at their research. More pages and surveillance logs were added to Yoder's GRU folder—but Yoder was no spy. While he was always given extra attention when he entered the snowy borders of the Union of Soviet Socialist Republics, his work truly was the work of God. Even the Russians came to realize that.

In a country where officially religion did not exist, even the hard Soviet system knew better than to try to eradicate it totally. Their leaders maintained control, and as long as the people went along, the leaders were more than happy to let the hidden services continue. Larry Yoder helped those struggling ministers and priests to spread the Word as he could.

Meanwhile, back in America, a storm was building within the halls of the headquarters that employed him. This storm would roll in and build into a raging tempest. The battles would be fought within the political halls of every church in America. The conservative elements within those churches would join together, set aside their individual differences, and organize for a takeover of the system at its core, to reform it back to a stronger fire-and-brimstone way. Few outside the protected world of church politics had any idea of the war that had begun at that time.

It really was war. It raged throughout the official buildings that housed the leaders. The storm spread across the seminaries, and the faculties and administrations took sides. At denominations' annual conventions, the war was fought aloud in rhetorical battles. The national media finally became aware and took time away from putting on their makeup to report the headlines.

This war was well into its fourth year by then. Battle lines were long in place, and the first blood spilled had long ago been absorbed back into the earth again. The conservative elements prevailed. Slowly their changes took effect. Careers were destroyed for political reasons, regardless of the religious convictions or abilities of the fallen.

Larry Yoder had certainly seen war, but, being abroad, he had been sheltered from this one. There was not much he could have done in those battles, anyway. This had been a war of generals, and he was but a private again.

He had been called back to the United States. Those who had hired him had already been removed by the victors. Yoder was cut loose: Those who had been under the wings of the vanquished were guilty by association. Informed that another, more qualified man would be replacing him in Europe, Yoder had to leave the job he had truly enjoyed.

He wandered for a bit before deciding to become a local pastor. He found a small church that wanted to hear the Word more than it cared about national politics. Yoder threw himself into the task. He was good at it. Very good. His soul was warmed every time he spread open the large Bible his grandfather had handed down to him to begin one of his Sunday sermons. His strength grew. He was coming home.

Then, on a rare vacation to Florida, he heard about a small church in Belle Glade. The local pastor had been chased away. The town's Southern Baptists had no shepherd for their flock. Larry went there and checked out the situation. It was true. The church was vacant on Sunday; slowly, entropy was having its way with the building. The harsh South Florida humidity and storms hacked away at God's house. This was not right, to Larry Yoder.

He prayed and thought about the situation. On his last day of vacation, he went to stand on the grass of the church grounds and stare for a final time at the dilapidated structure. It was then that his prayers to God were answered. For some reason, he had put on his collar that day.

An old woman, dressed in clothes no Goodwill would accept as a donation, approached him.

"Are you the new pastor?" she asked meekly, seeing his collar.

He thought a moment before answering.

"Yes. Yes, I am," he replied. "I'll be back in two weeks. My first Sunday service will be then, ma'am. Please tell your friends."

Yoder went to his old church and preached his final sermon to his beloved flock. He broke the news that God was calling him to another job elsewhere. Then he packed his few belongings and boarded a Greyhound bus. He ended up in Belle Glade.

He felt that all of his life up to that moment had been preparing him for what lay ahead.

Larry Yoder had found his home.

God's will be done.

CHAPTER 6

Check all magazines before going on an operation, to

ensure they are clean and properly loaded.

—POI 7658 Special Forces Combat Manual ROV 1970

Now that Ted Hickman knew his mission, he pre-pared for it. The first thing any good soldier does is get maps. He found those at a local well-stocked bookstore called Vero Beach Books. The helpful Sheila Grange led him to the map section, and Hickey had his pick from among the many there.

Along with the basic Florida road maps he found a detailed, inch-thick spiral-bound Rand McNally atlas of Palm Beach County. Belle Glade sat on the far edge of that county. He paid for the maps and some local Florida history books with cash.

After lunch—the fish they'd caught that morning—Custer had rolled into his wood-paneled office with Hickey in tow. As

Custer opened a hidden panel, Hickey stared up at two large-mouth bass mounted on plaques on the wall. Custer rolled over in front of a floor safe.

He spun the dial around and pulled the handle, freeing the heavy steel door. He reached in and removed stacks of cash and a slim blue passport. He turned his wheelchair around and threw the money onto the top of an antique mahogany desk.

"There's five thousand there, Ted," he said. "I don't need any receipts. Here's the combination to the safe if you need more and I'm not around." He handed over a slip of paper. Hickey would memorize the numbers, then destroy it.

Custer opened a desk drawer and pulled out brand-new Visa and American Express credit cards and added them to the stack.

"Your new identity, Ted." Fred smiled.

Hickey took the cards and passport and examined them. They were quite real. The passport had been issued by the U.S. government. The credit cards had been sent from their respective companies. Custer had done all of this work ahead of time, expecting that Hickey would take the job. Custer's money and contacts made things move when he needed them to.

"Nick Devlin?" Hickey asked. "Smith was already taken?"

"Hey, I'm a sucker for a good movie," Custer replied. "Besides, the only thing fake about those is the name."

Remembering something else, Custer opened another desk drawer and handed over a new cell phone to Hickey.

"Your new telephone, Mr. Devlin." He smiled. "Even takes pictures. Don't you love technology?"

"I'll figure out how to use it," Hickey commented. He had used military satellite phones before, but he didn't own a cell phone. That was for the younger crowd. He would master it soon enough. Having a camera on recon had certain advantages.

"Now, if you will remove those two bass from the wall, Mr. Devlin." Custer liked ribbing Hickey with his new name.

Hickey gave him a questioning look, but he lifted the plaques off the wall, uncovering two wooden pegs.

"Now, if you would please lift upward on those two pegs at the same time, sir," Custer directed.

Hickey was surprised when he lifted up on the pegs and an entire four-foot section of the thin paneling went up with them.

"Now, just bend the paneling a bit toward you and pull it away," Custer commanded.

This done, a four-foot-wide, six-foot-tall hidden compartment was revealed. It wasn't deep, but it didn't have to be. There before him was an impressive array of handguns and rifles waiting in the secret alcove.

A pair of Colt .45s and a .357 Python. A Smith & Wesson .44 rested next to a Browning High Power 9 mm. There was the newest Army-approved sidearm, the Beretta 92F. The Chinese AK-47 and a Russian SKS shared the space with a classic World War II M-1 Garand. A beautiful Thompson military machine gun rested there as well. Also an efficient, deadly Heckler & Koch MP5A sat there, the preferred choice of special forces and police units all over the globe.

"The art of camouflage," Hickey noted, impressed by the stash. He set the cover for the false panel aside and moved down a bit to examine the entire wall. He saw nothing that would give the space away. He went back to the weapons.

"An architect or builder measuring the two rooms might notice the discrepancy and figure out that there was an extra foot to the wall," Custer commented, "but a random thief would hit and run, never seeing the good stuff."

Hickey saw a true gem and carefully lifted a German 9 mm Schmeisser off the wall. He held it up and examined it in the light. It was beautiful, still retaining the original factory protective grease from World War II.

"Isn't a fully auto machine gun illegal these days?" Hickey asked.

"Not if you have a Class Three license," Custer replied. "Money talks, Mr. Devlin."

"I feel like James Bond." Hickey smiled. He put the German machine pistol back. He would have no use for anything like it on this assignment.

"If you want a gun, take your pick," Custer said.

"Well, I'll just take one of these," Hickey replied, lifting one of the old Colt .45s from its mounting. He could more than handle himself, but a handgun was sometimes useful in a pinch. The Colt was a proven and worthy weapon.

"That's unregistered, by the way," Custer noted. "I had to give them the serial numbers on the Schmeisser and the Thompson, but other than that, what the government doesn't know won't hurt them."

Hickey pointed the Colt away from them both and to the ground. The weapon felt good and familiar in his hand. He slowly pulled the slide back, locking the breech back open. A red plastic round rolled out onto his palm.

"Dummy round," Custer commented. "Not a live round in any of them. I have the ammo in another part of the house in a gun vault."

Ever the professional soldier, Hickey checked the empty clip himself. He examined the red plastic fake round before sliding it back into the chamber. He freed the safety with his thumb, and the slide slammed forward into place, the hammer now cocked back. Hickey pulled the trigger, and the hammer fell on the dummy round. There was no explosion.

"Smart" was all he could think to say.

He stowed the gun in his room, and then he and Fred went out and tested the new American Express card by purchasing a low-mileage Jeep Cherokee for Mr. Devlin. Smelling money in the vacant month of June, the salesman didn't even question the card. They drove away clean.

"I hope that bill isn't coming to your address," Hickey noted as they rolled over the hot summer pavement.

"Not in this life," Custer answered. "No, everything connected to Mr. Devlin is going to a Cayman Islands bank. They keep an account, opened in cash euros, mind you, for a Caymans corporation. That company is owned by a Nevada corporation, which in turn is owned by a Delaware corporation. Its shareholders are a couple of grave-marker names. Let anyone chase through that mess. They won't find me or you, Ted."

"I thought you were a Boy Scout, Colonel."

"Not on this one." That cold tone returned.

"Well, you went all out."

"I always do, Ted. I always do."

"How long did it take to set this all up?" Hickey asked, curious about this new side of his commander.

"Not that long, really. Most of it was done over the Internet by a smart young woman named Weegee. She knows how to cover her tracks. Sterling and I took his boat over to the Caymans with the cash. The rest was easy. The hardest part was getting the damn cell phone. Those credit checks were tough."

They drove back to the beach house, and Hickey was presented with a thick history of Belle Glade, Florida, to which three people had contributed. It had been rooted out from the vast maze of the Internet by the elusive Weegee, a retired *Miami Herald* reporter, and a Miami private detective.

Using a brand-new laptop, bought hot off the streets of Miami with cash, Weegee had settled into a luxury South Beach hotel as Mrs. Stillman. Living on room service and Mountain Dew, she had ignored the raging party zone and spent two days zeroing in on the data Custer had paid her to get. She burned it onto CDs, took a midnight walk on a long pier, and dropped the laptop into the ocean. The hard drive went with her, to be disposed of later, after she had more than ruined the memory disc in it.

Then Mrs. Stillman paid her sizable hotel bill with another

quite valid credit card, disappeared, and drove back up to her home in Vero Beach. She delivered the CDs to Custer and helped him print the material.

Still not satisfied, Fred Custer had used more of his contacts. He wanted everything he could get on the town, and he had the means to pay for it. He needed to know what the public couldn't access. His search led him to a retired veteran news reporter for the *Miami Herald* named Judy Wainscott.

She had begun her newspaper days in Cleveland on the *Plain Dealer* in the sixties. After her mother moved to Miami in the early nineties, Judy would come to visit her on vacations. After a hip injury, her mother had needed more attention, so Judy and her husband moved from snow-covered Ohio to South Florida. She was more than welcomed by the *Miami Herald,* as she had been nominated for the Pulitzer Prize for her investigative journalism. The *Herald* loved a good reporter who could wade through the hip-deep bullshit in which politicians and corrupt businessmen swam. She could weed out the truth, so she was hired.

She quickly learned the ropes of the new city and was back up to her old speed in no time. She finished her official newspaper reporter life and retired, but she still freelanced.

She could be trusted. Custer's local newspaper contacts gave him her name, and Custer and Geri went down and met with her.

At an expensive Coral Gables restaurant, Custer told her immediately why he wanted the information. That was one of the reasons she took the work. She liked people who told you the truth straight off. She could smell lies a mile away.

She knew that the man in the wheelchair hadn't told her the entire truth, but enough to make her care. Custer had kept the pending operation need-to-know, but he told her some things about Larry Yoder, and as she stared at the black-and-white photographs from a far-off time and a far-off Vietnam, she became hooked. Besides, she knew things about Belle Glade and wanted something to break right down there.

There was a lot hidden between the lines of the old magazine and newspaper stories and the police files she uncovered. She saw the connections but reported back only what she could document a minimum of two times. The rest she sent along as a bonus, thinking the smart man who hired her could also read between the lines.

All the material was organized by Fred Custer himself. The pages were bound at Kinko's into a presentable briefing document, the one he handed over to Hickey.

Ted Hickman spent three days digging through the material. He read the books and pored over the maps, sitting on that beach-front porch. He made notes and marks on the pages and prepared to drive into Belle Glade.

CHAPTER 7

Correct all team and/or individual errors
as they occur or happen.

—POI 7658 Special Forces Combat Manual ROV 1970

Sᴵᵀᵀᴵᴺɢ ʟᴵᴋᴇ ᴀ ᴊᴇᴡᴇʟ ᴏɴ ᴛʜᴇ Atlantic coast of Florida, Palm Beach was established long ago as a winter retreat for the ultrawealthy. Palm Beach showcased homes built majestically by people like the Goodyear family upon clean, white sands. Exclusive hotels such as the Breakers took care of the visitors and assured that the reputation of the perfectly built community remained intact. The sugar used by the elite in Palm Beach rolled in from Belle Glade.

Belle Glade was on the opposite end of Palm Beach County, away from the opulence. Until 1928, the small town was called Hillsboro; in that year, the town of five hundred incorporated and christened itself Belle Glade, taking for its motto "Her Soil Is Her

Fortune." It is said that this name was chosen in a write-in contest held in 1928 at the town's only hotel. Belle Glade got the most votes. No one remembers the second choice. Harking back to the antebellum Southern world, Belle Glade's residents saw their town as the belle of the Everglades.

Situated on the southeast shore of the vast Lake Okeechobee, where the Everglades begin, Belle Glade grew slowly over time, but not by much. For the most part, it remained a sleepy little town whose main industry was cutting the tall sugarcane each year and processing it into refined table sugar. To the people of Belle Glade, this was the original white powder, and it made fortunes long before the Colombians invaded Miami with cocaine.

One family rose out of that small town to stand atop the pile as the dominant controller of the region's vast resources: The Cole family was sugar in Belle Glade, Florida.

"Poppa" Cole had escaped from the rough coal mines of West Virginia into World War I. After Europe and the war, he didn't ever want to be cold again. He headed south as far as he could. He would have gone all the way to Miami, or maybe even the Keys, had his car not broken down in Hillsboro.

While he was waiting for the arrival from Miami of a sixty-nine-cent part, which no one in the sleepy town had available to beg, borrow, or steal, he explored. Moreover, he saw opportunity. So he stayed on in Belle Glade after that part arrived. He was hired onto one of the early sugar plantations as a supervisor.

Poppa Cole excelled at this task. He wasn't averse to using a fist or whip on the poor blacks or migrants who were used to bring in the crops. To him, these men were just tools. He earned their hate, but they knew better than to do anything about it in the twenties of the rural South. All the plantation owner knew was that his profits were higher than ever.

Poppa Cole was not content with a mere job, however. He had much higher aspirations. By making a truck full of the sweet white gold disappear from time to time and turning it into cash on the sly, or by shorting a man's pay, he built his nest egg. Then came the Great Depression.

One of the plantations was owned by a northern banker who had invested poorly. He needed cash to cover options, and he needed it fast. Poppa had cash, and he exploited the situation. He got over five thousand acres for pennies on the dollar.

Now, with his own land, he drove the workers harder than ever. No one stole from him. He caught one man doing that and, after beating and breaking him, Poppa Cole took him to a small wooden boat and out onto the lake. That was a trip from which the bleeding man never returned.

Cole beat his workers into submission. He also slowly, carefully expanded his domain. Some were bought out and others were chased out. The stubborn ones were burned out. The proper palms were greased to ensure that the officials looked away. A couple of owners who refused to sell . . . well, there was always the lake.

The only time Poppa Cole ever left Florida was to return to his home in the mountains of West Virginia. He took a bride. She was a sweet girl of sixteen when she was ripped away from all she knew and dragged to the South Florida swamps. Like his other workers, she was whipped and beaten into submission. To him, she was just another tool to use.

She gave him two boys, Fred and David, the results of what can only be called rape. After that, Cole was done with her; she was a broken woman before she was twenty, but her hearty West Virginia blood kept her going for another five years before she gave up the ghost and slipped away. To her boys she became just a fading memory or two.

By the end of the thirties Poppa Cole held the title to most of the important land in and around Belle Glade. He raised his boys and corrupted them, their innocence never having a chance to be seen. They grew up thinking that the workers around them were barely above the black dirt they worked. The police and local judge were just other employees to pay and tell what to do.

The family fortune grew. The boys grew into manhood and took their own wives and made their own children. Poppa Cole looked back with pride at what he had built. He had come here with nothing, and now he owned it all, and his boys, his beloved boys, would carry on the family traditions.

David and Fred Cole raised their own children as their daddy had raised them. Those children begat children, and they were raised in the family traditions. Poppa Cole was proud of them all.

Poppa Cole finally died in 1974 as a hurricane raged against the coast. Some said that nature's most powerful storm had come to claim one like her. Fred and David split the land on paper, but together they worked the family business to keep Poppa's legacy alive.

Then, in the sixties, the cheap labor they used began to assert itself. The righteous power of the Reverend Martin Luther King Jr. and the civil rights movement found its way even into the faraway cane fields of Belle Glade. The parents who harvested cane wanted better lives for their offspring than to stoop and cut all day, ending up broken at fifty to die an early death. Society began to allow these better lives.

These loving parents did everything they could to get their children away from the ruthless Cole family. Slowly, the future workforce of the region was sent away, and the Coles realized that something had to be done. The slaves had finally found a way to escape the masters, if not for themselves, then for their children.

The poorest of the third world, from Haiti, and the barely better off, from Jamaica, were brought in to work the fields, all of them illegal. Once again the Coles slid money into palms, and officials looked the other way. These refugees flooded in. Even the ruthless Cole tactics were not as harsh as the conditions from which these people came.

They came in waves during the late seventies and early eighties, lowering the wages below the pittance that the Cole family had allowed the locals. They jammed themselves into apartments, and those who could not afford even that lived in tin shacks on the edge of the lake. With them came the diseases of poverty. Belle Glade was one of the early vector points for AIDS in the United States. Drug-resistant TB flourished. There were other maladies there as well.

The refugees were a rough crowd, but the Coles were rough also. They hired tough men as needed to keep the new slaves in line. Every once in a while there was another trip out onto the lake. Powerful bass boats had replaced the wooden skiff Poppa had used, but the results were the same.

By the time Hickey was preparing to go into Belle Glade to see what had happened to Larry Yoder, Poppa Cole's boys were approaching their seventies. Their sons and daughters were in the prime of their late thirties and forties. As their grandfather and fathers had done, they ran Belle Glade, and they knew it.

That was the situation in Belle Glade, Florida, the day that Ted Hickman rolled into town.

CHAPTER 8

Do not send "same" or "no change" when reporting
team location. Always send your coordinates.
Keep radio traffic at a minimum.

—POI 7658 Special Forces Combat Manual ROV 1970

AFTER A QUIET LUNCH WITH CUSTER and Geri on the patio, Hickey left Vero Beach on Thursday, July 2. He wanted to be in the target area for the Fourth of July holiday. Even in this new America, things generally shut down on that day. He would be able to explore, with most everyone at home barbecuing chicken and burgers, drinking beer, and shooting off fireworks. It was a scorcher under the July heat as Hickey drove his Jeep into Belle Glade. Even the fully functioning Jeep air conditioner could barely keep pace with the Florida heat.

He hit Florida's main artery, Interstate 95, and headed south.

The traffic was light. He exited the freeway at Palm Beach, turning right on U.S. Highway 98/441, moving away from the exclusive Palm Beach areas. This road eventually paralleled the West Palm Beach Canal, draining the dirty water from Lake Okeechobee across the land and into the Atlantic Ocean, and became U.S. Highway 441 and state highway 80. He passed the airport and saw a group of parked Harleys outside of a little topless place called the Mermaid Club. Something there caught his eye.

Rising atop the back of the chrome backrest on one of the sturdy touring bikes, a bright red, blue, and white AA gleamed in the Florida sun. It was the symbol of the 82nd Airborne Division, the double A's meaning All-Americans. He kept moving.

He passed signs for Lion Country Safari. This little imitation Africa, like flypaper trapping flies, brought tourists in to see exotic animals from the Dark Continent. Hickey stopped at a Shell station next to the main entrance and refilled the tank of the Jeep.

He took a break by drinking a bottled Coca-Cola that had found its way from Mexico, where they still used glass for the bottles. A throwback to the sixties, it was sweet and cold, tasting different from the canned Coke made in the States. Hickey liked the Mexican version.

He drained the bottle and then rolled its cold glass on the back of his neck, cooling himself down. He tossed it into a recycling bin before getting back to business.

Highway 441/80 stretched out, and 80 cut south into Belle Glade. The houses and businesses became fewer and fewer, leaving the fields of sugarcane, corn, and rice, the main crops of the area. Oranges could be found in Indiantown close by.

Mr. Devlin's reservation for a weekend of fishing was at the Budget Inn, just north of the heart of the city. He could afford any hotel room, but the Budget Inn seemed to be the highest level of accommodation the city offered. There were two other hotels there. One had the promising name of Royal Inn of Belle Glade.

As he drove into the heart of the city and passed it, Hickey saw nothing royal about it. He made a U-turn and headed back to the Budget Inn and parked.

Before he checked in, he logged the position both on the Jeep's GPS system and on a handheld unit he had bought in Vero Beach. He dropped the handheld unit into the top of his new backpack, next to the loaded .45, and zipped the backpack shut. The pack, GPS, and expensive fishing gear in the back of the Jeep had been paid for in cash back in Vero Beach. The Jeep's GPS had been added by a good mechanic, with the help of a few Grants and Franklins.

A bovine woman, wearing 1960s-style cat-eye glasses and a green muumuu, didn't even smile as she checked Hickey in. She wasn't friendly at all, having been made to actually stand up on the slow weekday by the registering guest. Her cuckold husband usually handled these matters while she sat in their room, sucking ice cubes in the heat and watching cable TV. She had to handle the desk for the afternoon while he was away buying supplies for the weekend traffic of guests.

Without even a word, she slid the room key over for the ground-floor corner room Hickey had requested. Hickey wondered if perhaps the Royal Inn would have been a better bet. He took the key and went to his room.

Hickey had been in hotels all over the world. He had slept on mountains and in jungles. He had shared the huts of Afghan freedom fighters and Montagnard warriors. The Budget Inn wasn't the worst room he had ever been in, but it certainly wasn't the best, though it served its purpose. A bed, shower, and toilet waited; the sheets were clean.

Hickey unpacked his clothes and slid the thin particleboard drawers open. The .45 and four extra clips, with their fat lead domes waiting, went under his extra pants. He stripped and took a shower, surprised at how sticky the humidity had made him. Clean and cool, wrapped in a cheap white towel, he sat on the edge of the bed and picked up the cell phone. He punched up the number of the matching phone Custer had bought. Paid for in cash, it was registered to that mythical Cayman corporation.

Fred Custer picked up on the second ring.

"Hello?" The metallic, stiff digital signals broke up the human voice.

"I'm in the hotel," Hickey informed him. "I just have to start fishing now."

"Fishing" was the code word they had come up with for seeking information.

"Is everything all right, Nick?"

Hickey wasn't sure if Custer's emphasis on his fake name was another jab.

"Yeah," he answered. "Just fine. It's not even hot here."

"Hot" meant danger.

"Anything else to report?"

"Not now. I'll let you know after I catch a stringer."

"Stringer" meant information on Yoder.

"Talk to you later," Custer said. "Call if anything interesting comes up. Hope you catch a big lunker."

"Roger that." Hickey killed the connection. He didn't even know what a lunker was. He would have to ask.

Custer was busy also. He was still trying to locate that pastor who had been chased out of Belle Glade, the one Yoder had replaced.

Hickey would start exploring at dusk, a few hours away. He took a glass ashtray and placed it on the floor directly below the doorknob. Then he balanced two quarters on top of the doorknob. If the doorknob started to turn, the quarters would hit the glass with a clink and Hickey would be alerted.

He reached into his bag and dragged out a book he was reading: *Night Dogs*, by Kent Anderson. Custer had suggested it and given him the well-thumbed paperback. It was pretty good, Hickey had to admit, and he wasn't much on fiction.

He lay back and read until he fell asleep.

CHAPTER 9

Conduct a visual reconnaissance to familiarize yourself with
the terrain, select LZ's, E&E routes, reference points, record any
new trails in RZ and pick tentative PW snatch positions.

—POI 7658 Special Forces Combat Manual ROV 1970

IT WAS 8:00 P.M. AS HE drove away from the cheap motel. He hadn't brought the pistol. It might be a problem, having to explain a weapon if he got pulled over. He was hungry. Wahlan Chinese looked as good as anything, so he went there and ate in silence. To blend in and to look like the innocent tourist, he had grabbed a couple of local brochures offering guide services for outings on the lake. He read them while he ate.

After dinner, he got back on the roads, seeing the streets up close. He wanted to feel the place. He toured up and down the streets, absorbing things. When something looked noteworthy, he logged the point into his GPS system. He even took some pictures with the cell phone, surprised at how well it picked up the night images.

Hickey rolled slowly down Canal Street toward the lake. He knew where Yoder's church was. The old wooden church with its humble steeple sat on the edge of town, bordering the rough neighborhoods where illegal workers partied and rested at night. They had turned most of Canal Street into their private domain. Not even the Coles dared go into that section of town without damn good reason, and never alone.

Hickey eyed the slum houses and apartments that bordered this street, doors and windows open in an attempt to catch whatever breeze flowed by. Bright lights and loud music filled the night. He drove to the church, leaving the small third world behind him.

Hickey pulled into the gravel parking lot, shut off the engine, and cut the lights. With the full moon bathing the hallowed grounds in white light, he stared again at the decaying structure. If buildings could be haunted, here was a ghost. Reaching under the front seat, he grabbed a sturdy Maglite flashlight and stepped out into the night.

He walked the grounds, circling the building. He saw nothing of interest. He found a wooden door in the back at one corner. This would probably lead to the personal quarters or maybe an office inside. It was locked.

Hickey continued to explore the side of the building away from the road and shone the flashlight through a window. The bright beam danced circles across empty pews and a ruined pulpit. Hickey noted the rude graffiti painted across the wall behind that. Jesus, on His cross, lay sideways, ripped from the wall.

Hickey heard a car's tires rolling across the parking lot gravel. Twin headlights slashed a path across the far side of the building. He cut the Maglite off. Quickly, he moved around the side of the building and lowered himself to the ground. He barely stuck his head around the corner and saw a city police car coming to a stop.

He slipped completely back behind the building, sliding the Maglite under the church. Standing, he calmly walked around from the hidden side of the building and approached the police car. Its radio crackled across the night. Hickey was sure that Nick Devlin's plates were being run. The cruiser's door opened, and a heavyset man rose from behind the wheel.

The best defense is a good offense, so Hickey opened the conversation. "Hello."

"Howdy," the cop answered in a thick southern drawl. "What you doing out here? Where you from?"

"I'm visiting friends in Palm Beach," Hickey lied. "Thought I would do a little fishing. Heard you people have a lake around here."

"We got a lake, all right. Good fishing." The cop's hand rested on the grip of his pistol, his holster flap already opened. "It's over there." He thumbed away from town, using his free hand.

Hickey laughed.

"I asked what are you doing here. Around this here church at night."

"I'm looking for a church," Hickey responded, smiling. "I thought I might come in on Sunday."

"Well, this here church ain't open no more," the cop stated. "We have other churches, though."

"I noticed." Hickey continued the little wordplay. "But I'm a Southern Baptist. Always have been. What happened to the church here?"

The cop ignored the question. Officer Tom Wellman, like his father and his grandfather before him, was a Belle Glade police officer. The pay was decent, and the Coles added a little across the table often enough. For the most part it was a quiet town, with the only real problems generally coming from the cane workers' homes. The police went and cleaned up what needed cleaning up in the mornings. That left the afternoons for fishing. But he, not some stranger, asked the questions in town.

"Well, you'll have to get by with the Lutherans or regular Baptists, 'cause this church ain't open no more," Wellman reminded Hickey. "You got some ID on you?"

"Of course," Hickey said, reaching slowly into his back pocket and pulling his wallet out. He started to walk toward the cop.

"You just lay it on the hood there." Wellman stepped back, his arm shifting to get a more secure grip on his pistol. "Just step on back away into my headlights there."

Hickey did as he was told, playing the dumb tourist. Wellman picked up the leather wallet in his left hand and flipped it open, staring at the driver's license under the clear plastic.

"Mr. Devlin?"

"That's me," Hickey said, ready to move and take this cop down if he had to.

"Mr. Devlin of Moline, Illinois." Wellman's accent dragged the "oh" sound out before he paused. "How you like Florida, Mr. Devlin?"

"So far it's nice. It's a little warm for my tastes, but nice enough. I just want to catch some fish. You know any good guides I can hire?" Hickey asked, trying to change the subject.

"Well, now, you just go over to Slim's Fish Camp. It's over there on Terry Island." Wellman pointed toward the lake again, his tone softening on the subject he liked, fishing. "Ask anyone how to get there. And you tell old Slim that Tom Wellman sent ya. He knows the lake."

"Thanks, I will," Hickey responded.

Officer Wellman relaxed the grip on his pistol and stepped forward, handing the wallet back to Hickey.

"Well, you have a good night, Mr. Devlin. And I hope you catch you a big one." Wellman smiled.

"Thanks again." Hickey returned the smile and headed for his Jeep.

"Evening, now." Wellman closed the leather flap back over the pistol and snapped it shut.

"You, too, Officer," Hickey said, sliding into his Jeep and putting the seat belt on. He started the Jeep and rolled away, tipping a two-fingered salute to the cop from behind the windshield.

Hickey had figured correctly. As soon as Officer Wellman had rolled up, he had run the plates on the Jeep. Of course, nothing had come up. What Hickey did not know was that after his shift that night, Officer Wellman made a call. He dialed a number that had not changed in over forty years. He dialed the home of Fred Cole.

The Coles had let it be known that they wanted to be informed if anyone was seen around the empty church. Anyone. They had made that clear enough. So Tom Wellman passed on the plate number and Nick Devlin's name to the Coles. Their intention was to make sure none of the workers went there, but they would check that name out.

Hickey drove away from the church and saw the bright lights of a small shopping center. A Texaco station glowed on the corner. He pulled in to fill up the gas tank again. On the opposite side of the pumps from where he parked, a black-and-white county cruiser was also filling up. A large black officer rested his weary back against the side of the car as the gasoline flowed from pump to vehicle.

Hickey started his pump going and glanced over, noting the small USMC lapel pin on the officer's uniform. He stared up at the man's name badge. Hickey figured, correctly, that a county officer would not be on the payroll of the Coles. If he had known Officer Jackson better, he would have plied him with a lot of questions. Officer Jackson was no friend of the Cole family—he would have answered them.

Officer Jackson's grandfather often showed him the scars on his back that Poppa Cole had placed there. Jackson watched his father age before his eyes. Every day in the cane fields seemed to take a week from his life. Dirt poor as they were, Jackson's parents wanted better for their oldest boy. They saved what they could and got him into the local community college.

After two years and with straight A's, Jackson earned an associate's degree. He then escaped Belle Glade by joining the United States Marine Corps. He served proudly and with valor in Beirut and the first Gulf War. The Silver Star he humbly kept in a desk drawer at home was not handed out easily. He had more than earned it. He returned to his native Florida and was hired by Palm Beach County as a deputy sheriff.

He knew the history of Belle Glade, and he did not like it. He did what he could as a county officer, but even that authority had limits.

"How you doing?" Hickey began. Gnats were flying through the bright gas station lights.

"Just fine, sir," Jackson responded in a quiet tone. "And yourself?"

"Pretty good," Hickey replied. They lapsed into silence.

"You know what a lunker is?" Hickey asked, truly bothered by the unknown reference.

"It's a bass. Any good-sized bass." Jackson smiled.

"Oh," Hickey said. "A friend of mine told me to get a big lunker. I didn't know what he meant."

"That just means have good fishing around here."

"Well, that's nice," Hickey replied. He decided that he could trust the friendly ex-marine. "Desert Storm?" Hickey nodded at the lapel pin.

"Yes, sir. And Beirut," Jackson said, pride in his voice. The pump clicked to a stop.

"I saw Kuwait and Iraq," Hickey said, remembering long, cold nights in the desert. "Army."

"Yeah," Jackson mused. "That was some place, wasn't it?"

"Yes, it was." Both were silent, remembering their own moments there.

"Can I buy you a coffee, Officer?" Hickey offered.

Usually Jackson would decline such an offer, but something in his gut told him to accept this one, so he did.

They went inside, got coffee, went back out, and moved the cars. Jackson was on his dinner break, so he had some time. He usually skipped that meal. This was not only to stay in shape but also to stay alert on the second half of his shift. That was when things usually happened, and he didn't want a belly full of fast food draining the blood from his head and slowing down his thoughts and reflexes.

They sat and talked, each with the understood frankness that only veteran soldiers can share. It is an unwritten language.

Hickey mentioned the Coles in passing and saw something strong in Jackson's eyes, and it wasn't love. Hickey probed further.

Officer Jackson explained to the stranger that the Cole family, like a nest of hornets, was best left alone. Hickey pointed back up Canal Street, asking about the crime there.

"We get a call in there from time to time. The local boys usually handle it." Jackson sipped his coffee. "But mister, I've been in combat, and I won't go in there alone at night. Even during the day, we only go in pairs, with backup close by."

Hickey asked if Jackson had ever heard of Pastor Larry Yoder.

"Yes, I have." Jackson stared across the vacant parking lot of the shopping center. "My mother is a Southern Baptist. She used to go to his church. She liked his fire." He thought a moment and smiled again. "Though she says he can't sing to save his soul."

Hickey laughed at that. "Why is the church closed now?"

"That preacher just went away. He was just not there one Sunday morning. That's not the first time that happened." Jackson looked over. "What did you say you're doing here?"

"I'm here for the fishing," Hickey said. There was a long silence.

"Well, I hope you catch something good," Jackson said. He slipped his fingers into his top left uniform pocket and pulled out a card. "If you catch anything interesting, well, here's my number."

Hickey took the card and nodded.

"Well, I have to get back on patrol now. Thanks for the coffee," Jackson said. "You enjoy your time here."

"Nice meeting you, Jackson," Hickey said sincerely.

"You, too." Jackson started his cruiser and put it into drive. "You take care now," he added before driving away.

Hickey sat alone in the Jeep and finished his coffee. He drove by the church twice and, not seeing any police around, went back and retrieved the flashlight he had left behind. Then he went back to the hotel for the night.

He spent twenty minutes memorizing the information from Officer Jackson's card before tearing it up and burning it in the ashtray. He then flushed the ashes down the toilet.

CHAPTER 10

Tape the muzzle of your weapon to keep out water and dirt.

Leave lower portion slits open for ventilation.

—POI 7658 Special Forces Combat Manual ROV 1970

A FTER RUNNING HIS FIVE MILES ON the empty dawn streets of the just-waking town, Hickey punished his muscles with some calisthenics in a local park. His tendons flexed from the movement of the push-ups and sit-ups with which he assaulted himself. He ran again back to the hotel. He showered and dressed and decided to take the heavy .45 and extra clips along with him today. He slid them into the zippered backpack that everyone seemed to carry.

He ate breakfast at the local McDonald's—scrambled eggs served in a block shape, washed down with coffee. After that, Hickey decided to continue the subterfuge by driving out to

Slim's Fish Camp and pretending to care about fishing. He paid cash for a Sunday charter and got a receipt. He was hoping to be gone before that time.

He discovered that he was being followed. He had spotted a dark blue pickup truck as he had driven away from the town. Now the truck was following him as he drove from the guide's shop back into Belle Glade. Either these were amateurs or they just didn't care if he knew. A pickup truck is hardly the type of vehicle a professional would follow someone around in—especially one that rode an extra foot above the springs, designed for "mudding" the Florida swamps. Hickey pretended he didn't notice them.

He returned to the hotel, grabbed the backpack, locked the Jeep, and went back into his rented ground-floor room. He quickly moved through it, threw open the bathroom window, and dropped the backpack onto the dry ground outside. He followed and slipped into the waist-high yellow grass that bordered the back of the motel.

Hickey crawled through the grass until he was on the far edge of the area away from his room. There, he lay on the ground, ants already biting the tops of his hands; slowly, he moved his face through the grass until he could see the parking lot. He ignored the ants and watched the two men in the truck, hidden behind heavy tinted glass. They had parked near the front by the manager's office waiting for their prey, so they had had no way of seeing him slip out on them through his bathroom window.

Hickey slowly crawled backward, deeper into the covering yellow grass. When he had moved one hundred feet, he barely rose to a stooped crouch and legged it away from the motel. He never raised his body above the top of the grass. The yellow grass turned into fields of sweet sugarcane.

So the mere mention of the missing Yoder had brought the hounds out sniffing, he thought to himself.

When he knew he had moved far enough away from their field of view he fully stood up, stretching his back.

"You're getting old, Hickey," he reminded himself.

The strong smell of the brown tilled soil filled his nostrils. He took a deep breath and looked around. The sugarcane had risen only four feet. It would climb to six to eight feet before the winter harvest. Then the green outer coverings would be burned off, the blazing heat warming the night. This burning would prepare the sugarcane fields for harvest.

The three-inch-thick stalks would then be cut by hand. Men wearing aluminum shin guards would hack at the cane until all that remained was rooted spikes in the earth. The metal shin guards were to protect the men from the heavy machete blades used to slice through the bamboolike outer husks of the cane. A misplaced blow had cost many a man his life or a limb over the decades of labor.

Then the scorched earth, black from the carbon waste of the fires, would get a brief rest until the next planting.

Hickey stood and examined one of the meaty sugarcane stalks. He felt the stiff plant's fibers underneath his fingertips.

"So this is what it's all about," he commented to himself.

He moved off, away from the direction of the motel. He was used to doing his recon on foot.

He moved through the area, using the edges of the cane fields for reference points. He broke out of them by the Christian Day School and worked his way back into the heart of the small town. He logged the GPS when he felt it necessary, and he took pictures with his new cell phone if the target looked interesting enough.

He crossed back over South Main, well below his North Main motel, and entered the clustered houses and businesses of the town. He walked the streets, looking for targets of opportunity. When he reached the Victory Tabernacle of Prayer for All People, Hickey went into the small church. He was taking a chance that the servants of God might keep their faith stronger than the Coles' grip. He walked past the empty pews and sought the backroom offices of the establishment.

The Reverend Mark Janus looked up from his desk as Hickey entered the office.

"May I help you?"

"Maybe," Hickey replied. "I was wondering about a church down the road." He pointed in the direction of Yoder's locked doors. "Nothing against you, Father, but I'm a Southern Baptist. I'm just visiting for the weekend here, and I don't ever miss going to the Lord's house on Sunday. Now, why is that Southern Baptist church closed?"

Reverend Janus's head dipped, his chin resting upon his chest. He was pensive and quiet for a moment before he looked up and replied.

"I am a reverend, not a father of the Roman Catholic Church," he corrected Hickey. "The pastor of that church is away currently," he flatly stated.

Hickey did not know exactly what to make of that statement. "Will he be back on Sunday?" he asked.

"I do not know, but I doubt it. He has been away for three months now. There have been no services there in that time."

Hickey sensed sincerity in the opening line. So the man really did not know where Yoder was. He wasn't in with the Coles—or, if he was, it wasn't too deeply.

"May I?" Hickey pointed at a vacant wooden chair sitting in front of the minister's desk.

"Certainly," Janus assented, with his fingers rolling a welcome forward.

Hickey sat. "Sure is hot around here." He pulled a bandanna out and wiped his brow.

"We are known for the warm summers here in Florida, Mr. . . . ?" The question hung in the air.

Hickey shot his hand out and smiled like a salesman. "Devlin. Nick Devlin. Moline, Illinois." The lies rolled off his tongue with ease. The two men shook hands.

"And what brings you to our fair city, Mr. Devlin?" Reverend Janus queried.

"Lunkers," Hickey exclaimed, using his newly learned word.

"I heard you have some fat ones out there." He pointed his thumb over his shoulder in the direction of the lake.

Janus laughed. "Indeed we do, sir. Indeed we do."

"I've hired Slim's. We're going out Sunday." Hickey was seeding the ground with information that would keep his cover in place.

"The Lord's day, Mr. Devlin."

"He gave us fish, Reverend, and I intend to honor Him after services on Sunday by catching a few of them."

The minister laughed in earnest. "Well, since the Southern Baptists are currently not meeting at their church, may I suggest my humble house of worship for your prayers before you venture out onto the lake?"

"Well, I just may take you up on that, Reverend," Hickey replied. "You're sure that pastor won't be back?"

There was a cold pause in the Florida heat.

"I truly hope he does return. I pray for his return," came the response. "But I would not place a bet upon that outcome."

"Why not? A church needs a pastor."

"Indeed, Mr. Devlin, it does." There was another cold pause of calculated thought. "But around here, we have found that God's word is best delivered when one allows the business interests of the region to maintain a certain control."

"So that pastor"—Hickey pointed his thumb again in the direction of Yoder's church—"he didn't play along?"

"There were rumors among the clergy. We are a small group in a small town," Janus factually stated. "We do what we can here. But to do anything, we must live here first."

Hickey wasn't shocked. This wasn't the first man of the cloth to have an inability to move the mountain to himself. Men were just men when it came down to it, and most went along.

"It's not money?" Hickey asked. "I come from a pretty big congregation back home. We could maybe do something."

"No, no. It's not that," Janus assured him.

"But he's not coming back?" Hickey stated more than questioned.

"We pray he does, sir."

"Well, maybe I'll see you Sunday, then." Salesman Hickey stood and put his hand out.

"That would be my honor, Mr. Devlin," Reverend Janus stated sincerely, sharing another handshake.

"Until then . . ." Hickey smiled again, slipping one of the man's business cards into his pocket. He turned and left the small office.

Reverend Janus was not by nature a curious man, so he didn't follow and watch his surprise visitor leave the church. He didn't note that Mr. Devlin had no car. He made no calls when Hickey departed. He had believed the fishing story.

Hickey traveled back to his motel room using the path by which he had departed. As he had before, slowly he pressed his face through the waist-high yellow grasses. The truck was still sitting in the motel parking lot. It had moved, and now he was staring at the back of the truck. Hickey came up with an idea. It was a long shot, but it might pan out.

He slipped back in through his bathroom window and decided to take a nap. He would let his stalkers stew out in the heat of the Florida sun while he rested with the air conditioner blowing over him.

Then he would drive somewhere.

CHAPTER 11

"While on a mission, minimize fatigue
because tired becomes careless."

—POI 7658 Special Forces Combat Manual ROV 1970

HICKEY WOKE UP AND BARELY PEEKED out the window. The truck was still there. Smiling, he washed his face and dressed. He then called Custer, using the cell phone. This was their daily contact, which let Custer know everything was all right.

Taking his backpack, he exited the motel room. He didn't even glance toward the pickup truck as he started the Jeep and drove away from the motel, kicking up gravel before the wheels grabbed the pavement.

He quickly moved up North Main Street, away from the town. He watched in the mirror from the corner of his eye as the truck waited a moment before following. Hickey found 441 again and headed back toward Palm Beach. Thirty minutes later, the sun was beginning to drop in the west as he turned into the parking lot of the Mermaid Club with its promises of topless delights. Hickey was lucky. His idea might work out. The bikers were there. He parked his Jeep.

The holiday weekend meant free time, and the riders were just warming up for the long weekend in their favorite club. Hickey noted that unique AA atop the back of one chopper and stepped into the club's cheap lights. The truck had followed and parked in the lot outside. The drivers were unsure whether they should follow Mr. Devlin in.

It was their thirst from their long vigil that finally made the two men talk each other into going into the club. The Coles had ordered that the stranger be followed, but sitting outside in the hot July sun for hours had tested the abilities of these local thugs-for-hire. Plus it was the Fourth of July weekend.

Dammit, they should be at home sipping whiskey and getting ready to hit the lake in the morning for some serious drinking and fishing, not having to follow some Yankee around the area.

They decided following the man into the bar would not be against their orders, and a Bud or two sounded good about now. As they debated going into the club, Hickey was already establishing relations with the leather-clad bikers inside.

The gaudy red and blue lights of the club interior threw a proper tone across the bar. The Mermaid Club was perfect for where it sat on the edge of the Palm Beach airport. Stranded travelers without the means or desire to cross the freeway into Palm Beach could sneak inside, checking over their shoulders even though they were a thousand miles away from home.

Slipping wedding rings into pants pockets, they could indulge in beer and glance from afar at the naked women's bodies. These were the women wayward men wanted but most never spoke to above the chest level. The travelers never had a chance with the dancers, and the women were experts at getting an extra twenty or two out of the deal.

Both parties got what they wanted.

For the bikers, based in Lake Worth, this was home turf. They would unwind here from the week's dull work before hitting the backroads and highways of Florida, letting the wind flow through their hair as they cruised on their Harleys.

There was a baker's dozen of them, men and women, sitting at a couple of tables and at the bar away from the main dance area. They sipped cold Bud and Miller beers, not getting drunk but just lubed right before they headed out to tour with their bikes. A couple looked at Hickey, including a large man with a fading tattoo on his forearm. He had AIRBORNE ALL THE WAY needled into his skin, and under the words the distinct wings a paratrooper earns. He was the right age. Hickey had his man.

Thinking him yet another stranded air traveler, the bikers went back to their beers. Hickey ordered up a cold Miller longneck. After sitting a few moments and watching a dancer nicknamed Bunny gyrate her hips, Hickey headed over and pulled a chair up next to the big biker. The man looked over.

"I couldn't help noticing your tattoo there." Hickey pointed with the cold longneck beer bottle. "Nam?"

"Fucking A," the man answered in a bass voice.

"Yeah, I thought so. Me, too," Hickey replied. "Kontum district mostly, '71 to '75. Special Forces."

The number of men who were in Vietnam seems to grow yearly. Of that group, the number of those who actually saw combat appears to exceed by far the total number of troops America ever sent to Southeast Asia. As a result, every real combat vet has long since met men who claim to have seen the shit but had hung out in college instead. Many who were in the military had served stateside and never gotten close to Southeast Asia.

It takes just a few short questions—true knowledge of an MOS or a unit posting or designation; the way the names of the villages out in the highlands were pronounced—for the real combat vets to separate the wheat from the assholes. Why some pretend to be what they are not no one truly understands. Still, some do try to fake it. They cannot fool those who were there. Hickey and the biker verified truths.

"'75? Shit, man, you were there at the end," the biker commented. "3rd Brigade, 82nd," he said, tapping his tattoo and smiling. "I got my wings in January of 1968, just in time for the unit to deploy to Vietnam. That was some serious shit, man."

"It sure was," Hickey said. "Need another beer?"

"If you're buying."

Hickey went to the bar and dropped fifty dollars on the bartender with instructions to take care of the bikers. Then he added fifty more, telling the woman that was for her. He returned and handed the man a fresh Bud.

The biker stuck his hand out. "Mike Rose," he offered in return for the beer.

"Ted Hickman," Hickey added, sticking to the truth. Here was a man he could trust. They shook hands firmly.

The two men from the pickup entered the club at this time. They tried to look inconspicuous and went and sat by the dance floor, where Ginger was now plying her trade. Ginger's real name was Susan, and the topless dancing paid far more than being a waitress as she made her way through law school. Hickey made sure he didn't turn to notice the two men who were following him.

"So, what do you do these days?" Hickey asked.

"Investment banker," Rose said, pulling a nice business card from his leather vest and handing it over. Hickey looked at it.

"Any hot tips?" he asked.

"Buy gold, brother. Hard times ahead," came the unexpected reply.

As Custer had done with the Miami reporter, Hickey confided in his new friend. He told him that he was looking for the lost fellow Beret Yoder, and even said he was using a fake name in Belle

Glade. The common bond of soldiering goes deeper then noncombatants can understand.

"Belle Glade. Shit, even we stay away from that dump. They don't like bikers riding through. Easier just to roll around that place," Rose replied. "You some kind of detective?"

"No. I just mustered out two years ago. Lifer."

"You were even one of those officers, weren't you?" Rose asked.

"Yeah, but no West Pointer," Hickey said. "My parents were married."

Both men laughed.

"I'm just trying to see what happened to my friend," Hickey commented.

"Well, good luck with that," the biker said.

"I have a problem right now, though."

"What's that?"

"You see those guys that just came in?" Hickey pointed, barely, with the top of his beer bottle.

Rose slowly looked around as if he were checking the dancer out.

"The two crackers at the table by the wall?" Rose asked.

"That's them," Hickey confirmed. "They've been following me, and I would like to lose them. You have any ideas?"

"Let me ask my expert," Rose said and turned away. He nudged a fellow rider on the shoulder. A tall man in steel-rimmed bifocal glasses turned to face Rose. His once fiery red hair was a graying ponytail that went down to the small of his back. He and Rose whispered. The man's name was Anthony Smith. Only a few could call him Tony. He was a master with a knife.

Smith had also fought in the sixties. Unlike Rose or Hickey, he had fought his war on the streets of America. He had been at the core of the student antiwar movement. He and millions of others had forced Washington to change its polices.

The war Smith had fought had climaxed in Chicago in 1968 during the Democratic National Convention. There, thousands of protesters had been beaten, gassed, and arrested in front of the hungry news cameras that carried the moment of truth to televisions across the nation. Now Smith was a dealer in original art from the period, specializing in underground artists such as Crumb and Shelton.

The two bikers conferred.

Rose turned to Hickey. "You know what they're driving?"

"Yeah. A blue Dodge pickup. It's got one of those raised suspensions for mudding." Hickey then added, "Big sticker on the back windshield says I'D RATHER BE FISHING."

"Well, those boys might have a hard time following you with four flats," Rose mused.

"They just might," Hickey said.

Rose turned and gave the information to Smith. Smith slipped out the front door, unnoticed by the men from the truck, who were watching the dancers more than they were watching the man they were supposed to be tailing.

Hickey and Rose shared war stories, and Hickey told the biker that he would get his business card to a friend in Vero Beach who liked spreading his investments among former soldiers. Hickey then tried to hand Rose a couple of hundred-dollar bills for the service.

"No charge, man," Rose said, almost insulted, tapping his Airborne tattoo.

"Trust me," Hickey said, "this means more than the cash. This is just gas for the bikes."

Rose thought a moment before accepting the money.

"Fair enough," Rose said.

"Hoooah!" Hickey smiled.

"Airborne all the way." Rose grinned and winked.

Smith glided back into the club and nodded to Rose. The two thugs hadn't noticed a thing. Smith had used his sharp knife to sever the air valves on the big truck. It was far easier than trying to cut through the tires themselves and had the same effect.

"Well, I have places to go," Hickey said.

"Good meeting you, brother. Take care, and good luck." Rose meant it.

They shook hands; Hickey stood, walked to the bartender, and pressed two hundred more dollars into her palm with instructions. The bartender, told that it was one of the two men's birthday and that Hickey wanted them treated to table dances, sent the cash along to the dancers, who soon had the men surrounded. He had added another fifty dollars for the bartender.

Hickey slipped out the door and made his escape. Surrounded by the seminude women, the pair never saw Hickey leave.

He drove quickly back to the town of Belle Glade. The night had completely filled the skies. Hickey drove straight to Yoder's abandoned church. He wanted to look around. He drove past the silent structure and found a dirt road a hundred yards past its parking lot. He cut onto the brown dirt road and shut down the headlights. Driving far enough that his Jeep couldn't be seen from the main road, he parked at a locked gate in front of a field and slipped out of the vehicle.

Backpack secured over his shoulders, Hickey duckwalked through the half-matured cane, smelling the sweet green aromas. He stopped at a triple wire fence that bordered the back of the church grounds, silently watching for five minutes before moving out, making sure that no one else was around.

Hickey slipped between the wires and, staying low, quickly covered the short distance between the fence and the back of the church. Again he looked through the church windows at the moonlight-covered pews inside. He glided around the side of the white wooden boards of the church to the back of the building and the small door.

He popped the lock with a long screwdriver he had brought along. The old wood splintered easily from the force. Hickey slipped inside and closed the door behind him. He stood letting his eyes grow accustomed to the darkness. He slid his hand into the backpack and brought out a small LCD flashlight with a clear red lens cover. This was the best color for vision at night, and the shielded lamp would be almost invisible even if someone were outside looking into the church.

Hickey began to explore the monklike quarters. There wasn't much in the room: a cot, a small desk, a hard wooden chair. A few modest clothes were carefully hung in a small closet. Hickey moved the red beam around the room and discovered the only excess in Yoder's quarters: The red light danced across thick, serious religious books that filled two waist-high bookshelves. These were expensive, and Yoder had mail-ordered almost all of them from the excellent Square Books in Oxford, Mississippi, which specialized in these small-print-run explorations of the Bible, among other fine books.

Hickey wasn't sure what he was looking for, but there might be something. He almost missed it, but there it was on the bottom shelf, pushed back, resting atop a twelve-volume set of Jesuit writings on the books of the Bible.

What Hickey had spotted in the flashlight beam was a 1966 paperback handed out to all U.S. personnel arriving in Vietnam. Measuring five by four inches, the slim 170-page booklet was called *Handbook for U.S. Forces in Vietnam.* They had kept one of those in the team house, often quoting from it with laughs as they drank beer and whiskey, unwinding after a mission. The part that always got them going was the warning for U.S. troops to stay at least fifty meters behind the barrier wire to "prevent damage from VC-emplaced claymore mines."

Neither the VC nor the Chinese who supplied them made claymores. Those were U.S. mines, which the VC sappers would often turn around before attacking a camp. Then the sappers would disappear away from the camp and fire in a few rounds. When the Americans fired off the claymores, sending hundreds of deadly steel balls into the air, they would be striking against themselves. Charlie was smart.

Hickey pulled the small book out and flipped through it. He saw Yoder's messy scrawl on many of the pages. When he spotted the word *danhtu* he knew he had found something. He slipped the book into his backpack.

He finished exploring and found, in an old Cuban cigar box, Yoder's dog tags and medals. Hickey also added these to his backpack. Finding nothing else of interest, he exited the church and snuck back to his Jeep.

He grabbed a gas station sandwich and some chips and a neon blue Gatorade before heading back to the motel. The truck with the two men was not there. Once inside his room, he ate quickly and then explored the notes Yoder had left in the handbook before clicking off the light and going to sleep.

CHAPTER 12

Check all team members' pockets prior to departing homebase
for passes, ID cards, lighters with insignias, rings with insignia,
etc. Personnel should only carry dog tags while on patrol.

—POI 7658 Special Forces Combat Manual ROV 1970

WHILE HE WAS RUNNING HIS STANDARD five miles, Hickey thought about the notes Yoder had left in the old Vietnam handbook. Yoder had used a fairly simple method to secure the information. His notes were in Vietnamese. Anyone looking in the book, if he could get past Yoder's chicken scrawl, would find that unique language and probably think that it was all war-related material.

As written languages went, Vietnamese was fairly new. It had not become the official language of all of Vietnam until the Geneva Agreement of 1954, which also split the nation into North and South. The language, known as Quoc Ngu when the team was in

Vietnam, had been developed by Portuguese Jesuit missionaries in the seventeenth century. They had romanized the local language so they could teach their prayers to the people they sought to convert.

The first official dictionary of this new written language was published by Alexandre de Rhodes in 1651. But it was not until 1884, after thirty years of war, when the French took over Vietnam and made it a colony, that an attempt was made to make Quoc Ngu the official language of the land. The French wanted to Westernize the Vietnamese people, to purge the heavy Chinese influence out of their new colony. This Chinese influence was rooted deep, dating back well over one thousand years. The Vietnamese, always the rebels, had rejected these attempts by the French. It took until 1954 and that agreement in Geneva to make it the true official language of the divided nation.

What had caught Hickey's eye in the dark church was the word *danhtu*. "Coal" in Vietnamese is *danh tu*. Yoder had brought the two separate words together when he wrote of the ominous Cole family of Belle Glade.

Hickey had worked hard to bring his knowledge of the language back through the fog of years, and in the end, he had managed to hammer out the main thrust of Yoder's words.

Yoder had indeed started to become successful at getting many of the workers not to labor on Sunday. This was of no major consequence until the harvest was ready. Nothing was allowed to interfere with that burning of the cane and its harvesting. When half of two supervisors' workforce had not shown up one Sunday, the Coles were alerted.

Two of Poppa Cole's grandchildren visited the church the next Monday morning. Yoder was alone in his room, reading the Sermon on the Mount. The grandchildren hinted at potential problems if the sermons continued to bring a drop in production for the family business.

If Yoder hadn't been reading Jesus's Sermon on the Mount at

that time, the two grandchildren of Poppa Cole might not have left that room without some broken bones. Yoder, containing his anger like a steam engine with a broken valve waiting to blow, just asked them to leave.

He noted the next Sunday that many of the workers had not shown up for services. After the services he went and visited three of those families. The bruises and one broken wrist attested to the willingness of the Coles to enforce their dictates.

Yoder's sermons grew more muscular after that, and the Coles' tactics rose to meet them.

Yoder was hopelessly outnumbered, but then, "so was David against Goliath," Yoder had commented in his scrawl. He prayed more and continued the fight. So while Yoder checked that rising steam within himself by making his only weapon the Good Book and the Word, the Coles had no problem upping the ante on the new pastor. He wasn't the first man of the cloth they had dealt with.

Yoder's tires were slashed. Warnings were found painted on the side of the church for all to see. The final insult was that slaughtered chicken, its blood desecrating holy ground, evil sacrilege written in red blood across the back wall. That was when Yoder had e-mailed the last message to Custer and gone off to confront the brothers who now headed the Cole family.

Yoder went to see Fred and David Cole. Poppa Cole's prodigies were approaching their seventies, but they still ran the operations with an iron fist. Yoder set out to see them on a Saturday morning at the Belle Glade Country Club, knowing that the two aging brothers never missed a tee time on Saturday unless there was a hurricane.

Hickey let this information float though his head as he ran. He mixed it in with the briefing materials he had read written by Weegee, Wainscott, and the Miami private eye, Presnick. Presnick had managed to interview over a dozen people before he was chased away. It was the same story from them all. No one knew what had happened, but they suspected the Coles. The wife of the worker who had gotten the broken wrist had even made the sign of the cross when the Cole family name had been mentioned, as if she were warding off the evil eye.

Hickey knew he couldn't find out anything more than the three professional researchers Custer had hired. His military instinct told him the best defense was a good offense. He would go visit the Cole brothers on that golf course that very day. Hurricane Hickey had not landed yet, but it was a threatening menace off in the distance.

After he finished his run, Hickey showered and shaved before putting on the best clothes he had packed. He penned a quick note to Custer about officer Jackson and then another letter. He went to a drugstore and bought two padded envelopes and a magazine on bass fishing. Back in the Jeep he dropped the cigar box, the Vietnam handbook, Pastor Janus's business card, the biker's card, and his note to Custer into one envelope and sealed it. Into the other he dropped the magazine and a note to someone he didn't even know. That envelope he addressed to a rural Idaho zip code. He made up the name and address on the envelope. He used the Mr. Devlin fraud as the return address.

He then drove to the post office, checking to make sure he wasn't being followed, and parked and went inside. It was empty on the holiday weekend, but the vending machines were accessible. He slid Custer's package into an oversized Priority Mail envelope and addressed it to a Vero Beach PO box that Custer had rented. This envelope was stamped and mailed from inside the post office.

Another stamp went on the fake package. Hickey walked conspicuously to an outside mailbox and dropped the fake package in. He doubted the Cole influence reached into the local post office. Even though he could spot no tail on him today, he was being safe. If the Coles had corrupted the post office, they would find Mr. Devlin's package with the note talking about the fine fishing in Florida and hopefully miss the real one.

Hickey then drove to the Belle Glade Country Club.

The country club sat well outside the small town of Belle Glade. Canal Street became Lake Road as one drove away from the heart of town. The golf course sat on the end of that road, poised upon the very southeast corner of sprawling Lake Okeechobee. Co-designed by Gary Player, it was finished in 1987. It had eighteen holes and was open all year round. The Cole brothers had done much of the financing of the place. They were tired of having to drive far away to play the game that addicts many.

Hickey, unlike many military men, had never taken up the game. His running kept him in shape, and he had better things to do with his time than chase little white balls across manicured greens. It was a rich man's sport to the former New York City street kid.

It was just after 9:00 A.M. when Hickey parked the Jeep and got out. The brothers always started their game at 8:00 A.M. After that game, they would go get lunch at the Mexican place in town and then settle in and watch a movie, avoiding the afternoon heat.

Hickey figured they wouldn't be too far along the eighteen-hole course. He avoided the clubhouse and walked directly onto the clean, trimmed grass and headed out to find the two Cole brothers. He knew what they looked like from the newspaper and magazine articles the ex-reporter had given Custer.

They were alone on the sixth tee, dressed like two matching models for a Ben Hogan catalog. The only difference was the color of their shirts, tucked carefully into their expensive golf pants. Even knowing the brothers' history, Hickey had to admit that the fifties-style fedoras looked good on the potbellied, pale masters of Belle Glade, Florida.

Carrying the strong West Virginia blood of his parents, Fred Cole was tall, six feet three inches. At sixty-nine, he still stood erect and proud, his white hair a snowy peak above his head. David, sixty-seven, was shorter; his once dark hair had gone gray, and he was balding. That dark hair had caused a problem, as

Poppa Cole had suspected his innocent bride of an affair with one of the Hispanic workers when he first saw the boy. He questioned her.

That questioning had been in the form of a brutal beating behind their locked bedroom door. No answer the innocent wife of Poppa Cole cried out stopped the savage whipping—not even the lie of admitting to the false charge. It was on that night that Poppa Cole became finished with her and she began her final decline.

Fred had already fired his tee shot off and David was just putting his ball down onto his tee when Hickey found them. He saw their golf cart and sat down in it and waited. The two old men didn't notice the stranger as they concentrated on their opening salvo against the green fairway. They certainly noticed him after David's shot as they turned to get back into their cart.

"Who the hell are you?" Fred barked. "Get off that cart, boy."

The two men were not used to being confronted. Hickey remained silent.

"I said, get off!" Fred warned, shaking his fist.

Hickey sat, not even blinking.

The two men looked around as if the invader would disappear when they faced him again. Hickey waited.

"What do you want?" David Cole queried in a voice thinner than that of his elder brother.

"We have business." Hickey finally broke his glacial silence.

"We don't do business on the golf course," Fred said.

"You want to see us, you call the office." His brother seemed to finish the statement, his South Florida country drawl sneaking out of the man.

"This isn't about sugar," Hickey said flatly, bringing the sole of his shoe up to rest on the front of the golf cart. "This is of a more discreet nature."

"You that fella from out of town?" Fred asked. "What's the name?"

"Devlin." Hickey kept the lie going.

"The one the boys lost last night?" David turned to his brother.

"That's him." The eldest nodded. "Four flat tires. How did you do that?"

"I didn't do a thing. Must have been someone else." Hickey was cool. "I hear the crime is spreading out from Palm Beach these days."

Fred Cole snorted like a bull at the remark. "What do you want?" he demanded.

Hickey paused before speaking. "I represent a very wealthy man. A mutual friend of ours lives here. But no one has seen him in three months."

Hickey noticed that David Cole stiffened and glanced over at his brother, who remained untouched by the words.

"What does that have to do with us?" Fred Cole asked, as he tipped his hat up off his brow and wiped sweat away with a hand-kerchief.

"His name is Larry Yoder. Your company didn't like what he was saying from the pulpit. I'm not here to debate that. We just want to know where he is. That's all."

Hickey let the words sink in. "Nothing more. No questions. No one else gets called in." Hickey delivered the speech slowly. "We just want to bring him home. We don't care about what condition he's in. All we want is to get him away from Belle Glade."

"Well, we don't know anything about that missing man," Fred stated.

Hickey ignored the lie. "We'll pay, if that's what it takes. I repeat, we're not here to investigate. We are private people. We just want to see him home, no matter what his condition is." Hickey stood up from the cart.

"You heard my brother," David mimicked. "We don't know nothing."

"You know where to contact me." Hickey turned away. "Enjoy your game."

Hickey walked away feeling the eyes burning holes in the

back of his head. He went back to his Jeep and drove off, watching the green, open fields become the buildings and houses of the town again. From the time he left the Cole brothers, it took him thirty minutes to reach the motel.

The professional soldier does not fear other trained men in battle as much as he fears the amateurs. The professionals basically all ply the same skills and know what to expect from an adversary. It is the amateurs who do the unexpected, often catching the professional off guard.

Before Hickey even had the cheap door to the motel fully open, the handle of the wooden T-ball bat had slammed into his gut. Two men had been waiting inside. The thirty minutes had been more than enough time for the Cole brothers to call their eldest sons and get them to let the manager open his room to them. They were waiting.

Hickey doubled over, and before he could even react another hard wood bat slammed into his skull. He was out as his face hit the thin, worn carpet.

CHAPTER 13

Team encircled, the sooner you attempt to break out the
better chance you will have to do so effectively and
with the least amount of casualties. The longer you wait
the stronger the enemy becomes.

—POI 7658 Special Forces Combat Manual ROV 1970

HICKEY'S HEAD FELT AS IF IT were about to explode as
he came to. Slowly he opened his eyes, and the room he was
in came into focus from a foggy haze. The room was lit by one dull
lightbulb hanging from the center of the ceiling.

Hickey's shoulders ached. The reason for this was that his
wrists were padlocked in heavy metal cuffs connected by a one-
foot length of thick steel chain.

The chain was looped over a sturdy, inch-thick, rusty steel
meat hook, which was solidly mounted into a cinder-block wall.
This left him hanging by the chain, his feet dangling a good six
inches off the floor. He felt the pain in his shoulders from the

unusual position. His ankles were tightly bound by three loops of thick nylon rope.

A low clanking noise filled his ears. He looked around. The room was thirty by thirty feet with a large industrial pump filling the wall to his left. A diesel engine clanked away, pumping stagnant water in and out to some desolate sugarcane fields.

As Hickey turned his gaze away, his eyes came to rest on the back of a rail-thin man who was busy separating and organizing cold stainless-steel tools of some kind. The man was methodical in laying out his instruments.

Hickey could make out hemostats, surgical scissors, scalpels, hooks, clamps, forceps, dental picks, surgical rubber tubing, and more bizarre items. He saw a small pile of skulls in the corner. There were numerous animal skulls of different types and what certainly had to be more than one human skull in the pile.

Hickey knew that he wasn't the first person to be brought out to this charnel pumping station. He also knew that he had to move quickly if he wanted to live.

The thin man turned around and stared at Hickey, as if he had sensed his latest victim slowly coming awake. The man was wearing blue jeans, a black Nine Inch Nails T-shirt, and Vans tennis shoes. Hickey's eyes locked onto the man's gaze. He did not like the mania he saw behind those eyes. Even by the Cole family standards, this one was strange.

"Man" was a poor word to describe John Lee Cole. He was hardly a boy at nineteen. Skinny, with pimples, he lived on an almost exclusive diet of pizza and Dr Pepper. Like most sadistic killers, he had started out as a child torturing small animals. He would catch them and bring them out to the pumping station, away from civilization, and have his way.

He enjoyed the squeals the trapped animals gave as he inflicted slow pain and eventual death upon them. As he sliced through tendons, muscles, and bones, he marveled at the creatures' spasms and convulsions. More than once John Lee Cole had suffered bites or claw marks from the animals as they fought back. Any trapped animal, even a rabbit, will fight back when it knows the end is near. Over time, John Lee improved his macabre skills. He learned how to restrain the animals completely, as well as how to inflict the maximum amount of pain upon the poor creatures as he slowly cut their skin open and exposed the delicate organs of the inner body.

He had, of course, read all about those who had gone before him. Ed Gein, Albert Fish, Jeffrey Dahmer, and Ted Bundy were his role models. While other boys his age were following their Miami Dolphins or NASCAR heroes, John Lee was reading all the true crime books he could lay his hands on about serial killers. He reveled in watching Court TV when it covered his heroes. The Internet became a vast resource for new techniques or tools for inflicting pain to try out on his victims.

Those around him thought it was just some teenage phase and didn't think his long hours spent away from home were unusual for a boy his age. No one had any idea that almost all those hours were spent in the old pumping station on the edge of Cole sugarcane property.

He had taken his first human life when he was sixteen. The animals had become boring to the growing sadist, and with his new driver's license, he was able to escape the small enclave of Belle Glade. By studying those who had gone before him, he knew better than to strike locally. Late at night, he found an innocent seventeen-year-old hitchhiker who had been in a fight with her boyfriend at a party and left him there. She figured that she could hitch a ride back to Fort Lauderdale.

Her name was Cathy Arnold, and her face still appears on some milk cartons.

After picking her up, John Lee feigned car trouble and pulled over to the side of I-95. He checked under the hood, with cars driving by at 70 mph, then got back in the car holding the shop rag he had used. Cathy Arnold didn't know that John Lee had hidden a bottle of chloroform under the hood and soaked the dirty rag with it.

She fought, of course, but John Lee had a madman's advantage. Once she was unconscious he quickly drove her back to the pump house, dragged her inside, and soon had her tied tightly. He didn't leave there for over two days as he explored his new victim. He smiled as he opened her skin to explore her ribs. Her pleas and screams only drove him deeper into the mania.

When she was finished, he stripped naked and spread her blood on his skin and went out and danced in the midnight moonlight. Hardly sated, but knowing he could not do everything he wished, he dragged her body off deep into the canals that feed the cane fields. It was here he cut her head and hands off using a heavy surgical saw. This was done to prevent easy identification if the body was ever found. He then dumped the weighted torso deep into a backwater pond.

No one ever found his burial place for his victims.

He took the hands and put them into a weighted backpack and threw them overboard into the depths of Lake Okeechobee. He kept the skull; this he stripped clean by using dermestid beetles he ordered through the mail. Then he hid everything and waited to be caught. At night he would bring her skull out and feel its texture under his fingertips as he lay awake in the dark.

After three months, John Lee realized that he had gotten away with his crime. The hunger to kill a human soon grew within him again. A thirteen-year-old Haitian daughter of one of the cane cutters was miles from home and close to the pumping station one day when he went to check on his secret place. Everyone assumed she had wandered off too far into the swamp and a gator had eaten her. The lives of the poor are cheap in most places, and no one looked too hard.

It was with his third victim that he was caught by the Cole family maintenance man who had come to inspect the pumps. The man knew better than to go to anyone except the two eldest Coles when he saw John Lee torturing the half-naked boy. John Lee had met the boy at a local McDonald's, tricked him into the car, and used chloroform on him. John Lee had no sexual preference; he wanted to see how a male of the species would scream under his tools.

The elder Cole brothers kept family business within the family. That the boy was willing to torture—well, such a skill was rare and quite useful to men like the Coles. They had a conference with the boy's father. As long as John Lee did what they wanted sometimes, he could do whatever he wanted in the pumping station. He was warned to be careful and not to take any more locals for his experiments.

So after Hickey was captured and the elder Coles wanted to know exactly what he knew and who sent him, he was brought to the pump house. His suitcase and backpack were dumped in one corner while he was cuffed, chained, and hoisted up, and John Lee prepared.

John Lee's father, James Cole, waited outside in his truck. James Cole was the younger brother of Jenson Cole, the eldest son of Fred Cole. He kept his radio on to cover up any screams as the boy did his work. John Lee's father had sat out in that truck before.

"You're awake. Good." John Lee smiled, looking up at Hickey.

Hickey's training took over. Give them nothing for free. The more they had to work on you, the longer you had to escape. He placed his heels against the wall and tried pushing upward to loop the chain over the hook. The eight inches of hook above the chain was too far.

"Oh, that won't work." John Lee smiled, walking toward Hickey with one arm behind his back. "They all try that."

Hickey relaxed and went slack to conserve his strength.

"Now, we are going to have a talk," John Lee stated. "I have a list of questions my granddaddy wants answered. And you will answer them."

"Go to hell," Hickey spat out.

John Lee didn't say a word. He grabbed Hickey's shirt in his right fist and pulled it forward. Then his arm came out from behind his back holding a beyond-sharp number 4 scalpel. He carefully placed this at Hickey's neck.

"You will die here, slowly, and begging for it long before the end. But before that happens, twenty hours or so from now, you will tell me everything I wish to know."

John Lee slowly slid the scalpel downward, cutting away Hickey's shirt. Then he placed the handle of the blade in between his teeth and held it there while he reached into his back pocket and pulled out a self-locking hemostat, closed the teeth down on Hickey's left nipple, and locked the hemostat in place.

Hickey clenched his teeth but didn't let out any noise. He had felt pain before. He made this new pain his friend. Pain was how you got through Special Forces training, and it was a constant companion for the professional soldier. Hickey wouldn't give up anything without a fight.

He started thinking of an old cadence song in his head to slip past the pain.

Who's the man in the green beret?
Makes his livin' in a special way,
Special Forces leads the way,
To make a brighter day!

The words ran through Hickey's head as John Lee pushed him against the brick wall by pressing his neck hard. Hickey was surprised by the boy's strength. He felt the sting of another hemostat jaw as it locked down on his earlobe. John Lee then took the scalpel from his mouth and made a light, three-inch incision on Hickey's chest, across the breastbone. It was not a deep cut. Just enough to break the skin and let the victim feel his blood leaving his body. John Lee knew better than to bleed out his man too soon.

John Lee released the grip on Hickey's neck and slid his finger across the wound. Then he held up his bright red blood-covered digit so Hickey could see it.

"There's about ten pints of that in you," cooed John Lee, "and I know just how much to let out before you black out. I'll do lots worse things before that happens, old man."

John Lee slid the finger across Hickey's cheek, smearing the blood there.

"Now, my granddaddy wants to know who sent you, and what you really know. You can make your death easy and quick. I would prefer a three-day session with you, but I have orders. You'll tell me what I want to know, one way or another. Within ten hours, you'll feel like it's been a week, and you'll be babbling like a baby."

John Lee paused and closed his eyes, then spoke. "Now, who sent you?"

Hickey wanted to lash out. He could have. He could have easily kicked his bound ankles out and sent the boy sprawling to the ground, but there was no point to it. Not yet, he thought. He took himself back to his boot camp days at Fort Bragg, running in the North Carolina heat. He again ran the old cadence through his head.

Who's the man in the green beret?
Makes his livin' in a special way,
Special Forces leads the way,
To make a brighter day!

While John Lee was a self-taught amateur, he was a smart one. He had learned some tricks. He pulled a short wooden dowel out of his back pocket and slammed one end of the blunt stick into Hickey's solar plexus, where the body has a large collection of nerve endings. Hickey felt the pain. He winced, but again he absorbed the pain. Nothing escaped his mouth.

"Who sent you?" John Lee asked.

Hickey knew he had to fight back. So he went after the boy's mind.

"I've been hit harder by a twelve-year-old Vietnamese," Hickey replied.

"Who sent you?" John Lee repeated.

Hickey felt the dowel slam down again in the same spot. More pain. Hickey swallowed it, refused to let it out of his mouth. He continued his counterassault.

"A twelve-year-old Vietnamese girl," Hickey responded, grinning.

John Lee balled his fist and slammed it into Hickey's face. Hickey felt his lip crack open and start to bleed. He smiled. He had scored a hit.

"I have some tools your girlfriend never had." John Lee turned and walked to his table of death.

Hickey knew it was now or never. He still had the best mobility he would get. Only God or Satan knew when the boy might use the scalpel to cut the tendons in Hickey's legs or someplace else, incapacitating him.

Again, as he had been trained, and as he had done so many times, Hickey went deep within himself.

"No" and "can't do" were not options now. He snapped his neck hard left, hearing the pop. He then brought his bound feet up and probed the wall under his heels for something, anything. He found it.

There was a small crack in the wall. Would it be enough? It had to be. Hickey would make it so.

While John Lee went through his inventory, deciding what to use next, Hickey pressed his heels down into the crack. His right boot heel took hold. One chance. One shot, but that was what he was trained for and ran five miles for every day. He had lived on less before.

"Special Forces leads the way . . ." Hickey shouted aloud now as he brought it all up from deep within him. All the running with rock-weighted rucksacks. All the dodged bullets and jungle nights. Hickey thought of Yoder, deep in the bush over thirty years ago. He thought of Yoder in the middle of a sniper attack as they were all hunkered down behind trees and berms, whatever cover they could find. Yoder's words flowed back through the corridors of time.

"Because he hath set his love upon me, therefore will I deliver him: I will set him on high, because he hath known my name. Psalms 91:14." Yoder had said this as the sniper's bullets whizzed around them, keeping them pinned down, until Winkler had flanked the man and put a three-round burst into him.

Hickey pushed upward with everything he had. He looked up at the chain links holding his wrists hanging from the eight inches of steel hook. He willed those links over that hook. Hickey pushed up off the wall, using his leg, back, and arm muscles to propel himself off of that hook, and he flew through the air.

He landed with a thud, rolled, and quickly was up. No longer immobile, the chains now a weapon, Hickey had become a threat.

John Lee heard the thud and turned. He was frozen for a second. None of his victims before had ever done anything but plead. John Lee's hesitation became his death sentence.

Hickey hopped closer, keeping his balance, poised for attack with the one-foot loop of chain hanging between his cuffed hands. He hopped forward again, closing the distance. John Lee got into what he imagined, from all the movies he had seen, was a knife fighter's stance, the scalpel ready in front of him in his right fist.

Hickey had trained and fought real knife fighters. "You watch too much TV, boy," he said, and he hopped still closer, careful not to lose his balance, closing the gap. "I'll give you one chance to live. Where's the key to these cuffs? Leave it and run."

John Lee's eyes went to his side. Hickey saw the key chain on the boy's belt loop. At least Hickey wouldn't be wearing cuffs out of here.

"Leave those and run, boy. Now," Hickey warned again.

John Lee chose to attack instead. He came at Hickey, thinking that a man with bound feet would be easy to take. John Lee Cole threw his weight forward and charged, swinging the scalpel. Hickey responded.

Instead of standing, Hickey dropped to the ground and rolled forward. His 210 pounds swept through the boy's feet as the scalpel sliced empty air. The boy's feet left the ground, and John Lee slammed face first into the dirt. Hickey didn't hesitate. He who hesitates is lost.

He finished the roll and came up on his knees, then jumped onto the boy's back. He slammed his knees down onto the small of his spine and heard John Lee scream. Hickey wrapped the foot of steel chain around John Lee's neck and pulled backward with all his strength.

Hickey crossed his wrists, twisted the chain, and pulled harder. He dug deeper. He thought again of Yoder.

John Lee lashed out, trying to free himself, but his weight was no match for Hickey's. He was shocked at having been on the receiving end of pain, too, and thus he was no match for Hickey's rage. Still, like a trapped animal, John Lee lashed out.

Hickey didn't feel the scalpel sink deep into his thigh as he pulled the boy's neck harder under the chain noose. He didn't hear John Lee Cole's neck snap as life left the insane boy.

Hickey didn't know how long he sat there atop the dead boy before he released the grip. He pulled the scalpel out and cut the ropes from his ankles. He then took the handcuff key and released the cuffs on his wrists. It stung him as he removed the hemostats and his blood returned to places it had been cut off from. He threw the hemostats aside.

Now free, Hickey examined himself. There was nothing serious except the wound in his thigh. He was losing blood, but the boy hadn't hit anything vital. He grabbed the surgical tubing and tied it off above the cut on his thigh.

Next he went to his backpack and opened it. The .45 was still there. He pulled the slide back, sending a round into the chamber. Then he went over and made sure John Lee was dead by sliding the scalpel through the boy's neck. The blood pooled in a black puddle in the dirt.

"See you in hell, kid," Hickey said.

Hickey looked at the metal door of the pump house. He didn't want to use it if he didn't have to. There might be others outside. He walked over and examined the open space on the other side of the pump. There was a gap there where he might slip out the back. He explored further.

There was enough room, and Hickey forced himself around and over the pipes as they sent dark water flowing into the cane fields. He dropped onto the soft mud to the side of the pond just outside the pump house. It was deep nighttime.

He slowly moved up the incline, staying close to the ground. He saw a truck. He slid back behind the corner of the building and waited, letting his eyes adjust to the darkness. He sat and listened to the pump grind away and the water flow. He slid back down the incline and followed the edge of the water until he was next to a cane field.

He moved into it and through it, flanking the truck. He crept up behind the truck and, crouching, worked his way up on the passenger side. When his left hand slipped down to his leg wound, he felt the blood on his pants. He was losing blood fast. Too fast. This was no time to delay. He was still in danger.

Hickey reached up and grabbed the truck's door handle and pulled it up. He yanked it open and stood, bringing the .45 up. John Lee's father never knew what hit him. He had dozed off to the sounds of the radio and groggily woke up thinking it was his son. He never heard the three bullets that slammed into him. He just slumped over dead.

Hickey looked around and saw no one else. He double-checked the perimeter. He had to do something with the bodies now. He dragged John Lee's father into the pump house and leaned both bodies against the large diesel fuel tank that fed the big engines.

Hickey then dragged his bag and backpack out and threw them into the truck. He made sure the truck had its key in the ignition and turned the motor over. He shut the engine down.

He went back into the pump house and found what he needed. A gallon jug of water. It would do. He dumped the water out as he walked back to the truck. He loosened the surgical tubing from his thigh and opened the truck's gas tank. He siphoned out some gas, filling the jug as he spat the gasoline from his mouth. When the jug was full, he yanked the tubing out and put the gas cap back on. He dug into his backpack and took out a lighter.

Hickey took the gasoline inside the building and looked until he found the diesel pump shut-off switch, slamming it down. A sudden silence engulfed the room. He then opened the diesel fuel tank and poured most of the gasoline in. Removing his shirt, he ripped a long strip from it and soaked it with the remaining gasoline. Then he threw the jug aside and pushed the gas-soaked rag into the top of the fuel tank on the pump.

It hung a solid two feet from the top of the tank. Hickey lit the bottom of the rag and ran. He figured he had a couple of minutes as he ran to the truck and started the engine. The tires dug into the gravel and spun for a second before gripping. Hickey headed down the short dirt road and then onto the paved highway that ran next to the pump house. He was well away when the explosion filled the rearview mirror.

It was late. Hickey looked around and saw the glowing numbers of the truck's clock. It was just past midnight as he rolled down the road. He spotted the highway marker for 441/80. He reached down and felt his leg. He was losing blood and his head was banging like that diesel pump, so he pushed himself more; he went again deep into his will. He turned right onto the highway and headed away from Belle Glade and toward Palm Beach.

He didn't remember pulling into the Mermaid Club parking lot and banging on the back door.

The bikers weren't there, but the bartender remembered him. Men who leave hundred-dollar tips are not soon forgotten. Hickey didn't remember pulling out his cell phone and punching Custer's number before handing the phone to the bartender and passing out.

A BUILDING STORM

CHAPTER 14

*A buddy system should be established in case casualties are
taken at night. Each man will take care of another man and his
equipment if one is wounded, injured, or killed.*

—POI 7658 Special Forces Combat Manual ROV 1970

H ICKEY WOKE IN A STRANGE BED. He ached. He hurt in
places where he had forgotten he had nerve endings. Something was buried in his left arm, and he reached over and felt a
tube that had been drilled into his vein.

It was dark in the room. A little light flowed in from the hall-
way. He lay there letting his eyes adjust to the silhouettes and
shadows. Through blurred vision, he saw pictures on the hall
walls. He was in someone's home. Custer's beachfront home. The
place didn't smell like a hospital or private rest home. Those
places smelled of either bleach or death. This place smelled of
home.

He saw a water bottle next to his bed. Taking it, he unscrewed the cap—amazed at how difficult that task was, how weak he felt—and took a drink. Before he knew it, he had drained half the bottle to quench his thirst.

He screwed the top back onto the bottle and leaned over, replacing it on the bed stand by his side. A green neon clock face glowed 3:12 at him. He willed his aches away, submitted to his need for more sleep, and closed his eyes again. He was back under within two minutes.

THE SUNLIGHT CUTTING THROUGH THE blinds greeted Hickey as he opened his eyes. Looking around, he saw Custer, reading a book, sitting by the bedside in his wheelchair.

"What you reading, chief?" Hickey croaked in a weak voice.

Custer didn't look up as he put a bookmark into the pages and closed the book. "*In Deadly Combat: A German Soldier's Memoir of the Eastern Front.*"

"I'll wait for the movie," Hickey replied.

"How you feeling?" Custer asked.

"Like I fought at Stalingrad, and on the losing side," Hickey replied. "How long have you been waiting by the bed?"

"Since this morning. Juanita told me you drank half a bottle of water last night."

"Juanita?" Hickey questioned.

"Your private nurse. I have three of them, 24/7, ace. Juanita has been working the eleven-to-seven shift." Hickey set the book down. "The doctor will be in this afternoon to check on you."

Hickey looked over and saw the clear tube running from his arm to a bag hanging on a metal hook. "They make house calls these days?"

"Some still do."

Hickey rolled the plastic tube between his thumb and forefinger. "How bad was I?" he asked.

"Not bad, but not good," Custer replied. "The doctors didn't know where you had been. All the ambulance crew knew was that there was a bleeding man at a strip club outside Palm Beach. A strip club, Ted?"

"That's Mr. Devlin to you." Ted returned the pseudo-name barb back at Fred. "I had some friends there."

"Well, the bartender spoke highly of you."

"I bet I looked good," Hickey mused.

"Pretty beat up. You collapsed after dialing the cell phone and handing it to the bartender. She spoke to me and then called 911. You were taken to Boca Raton Community Hospital, and they treated you while Geraldine and I drove down there. They stabilized you, and I arranged a private ambulance to bring you here. Then I hired a doctor and the nurses."

"How long have I been out?" Hickey asked.

"Three nights," Custer said. "Your concussion was the worst thing."

"Yeah, a baseball bat to the head will do that," Hickey replied. "And are there any warrants out on me from Belle Glade?"

"Should there be?"

"Depends on if anything was reported," Hickey stated.

"Not a peep," Custer informed Hickey. "I did some sideways checking down there. I talked to that deputy you told me about in your mailed package. Mr. Devlin was not wanted for anything. Not even the strange little fire outside the town with the two bodies they found in the ashes. What happened down there, Ted?"

Hickey paused, closed his eyes, and told Custer what had happened that night. They sat in silence for a moment when he had finished.

"Not a very nice guy, that kid," Fred thought aloud.

"Yeah, well, he won't be bothering anyone else," Hickey said with no emotion. He had killed before, and only a couple of those deaths lived in his rare nightmares. John Lee Cole would be no nightmare to Hickey.

"Is the sheriff looking into that place?" Hickey thought back to the piled bones in the corner of the pump house.

"No," Fred replied. "It's local police jurisdiction."

"Bought and paid for by the Coles," Hickey said.

They sat in silence for a while.

"So, now what?" Hickey asked.

"Well, you spoke to the Coles, and they aren't selling anything," Fred commented. "You feel up to some reading?"

"If it's interesting."

"It might be. It's a report." Custer brought a bound volume up from where it had been wedged in between his thigh and the side of the wheelchair. He handed it over to Hickey. "I found the pastor Yoder replaced. That took some doing. Then it was more difficult to make him talk."

"Scared?" Hickey asked.

"Very," Custer replied.

"I have feared only two things since I walked out of Bragg," Hickey commented. "God and a nineteen-year-old whore I met in Saigon once."

"Really, Ted?" Custer perked up some. "I don't think I've heard that story."

"I'll tell you sometime, Fred. But trust me, Uncle Ho himself would have run from her." Hickey smiled.

"Well, read the report, and if you're feeling up to it, some old friends will be here this afternoon."

"Yes, sir." Hickey saluted halfheartedly.

"I'll come get you for lunch." Fred rolled his wheelchair back and sideways and headed out of the room. "I have some guests to greet."

Hickey opened the report and started to read.

CUSTER HAD DONE HIS JOB. A private detective agency in the Twin Cities area of Minnesota had found the pastor who had fled Belle Glade and left his church empty. His name was Gary Cate, and he had run to a small town called Ray in northern Minnesota. There, close to the lake and deep in the woods, he had hoped to leave his failures in Belle Glade behind him.

One of the agency's men, Greg Ketter, had tracked him down and found him running a summer tourist RV camp. It was a desolate job most of the year, and that was fine with a former man of the cloth. He had given up on the Word and tried to send his demons away nightly.

The pile of empty Jack Daniel's bottles outside his cabin attested to his inability to fight them alone.

If Ketter hadn't been standing between Cate and the door, Cate would have run to Canada instead of talking, but talk he did. He let it all out, for two hours. It wasn't the threats or the warnings or even the light beating handed out to him in God's house in that faraway town that sent him fleeing. It was the midnight trip into the middle of one of the Coles' cane fields that made him run, never looking back.

Hogtied and gagged by two of the Cole henchmen, he had been thrown into the trunk of a vintage charcoal black El Dorado in what he knew was his final car ride.

After a fifteen-minute bumpy ride the car stopped, the trunk was opened, and he was thrown out onto the black soil of the middle of a cane field. No words were spoken until after the gasoline had been poured over him.

Jenson Cole, eldest son of Fred Cole, personally lit a road flare and inched it toward the trembling man. Cate tried to move away, but a hard boot into his spine froze him to the spot.

Jenson Cole asked him one question. Was he going to pack up and leave tomorrow morning? Gary Cate cried as he nodded yes. He might live.

Jenson Cole told him what would happen if he wasn't gone by noon.

"You'll be back out here tomorrow night, and I'll drop the

flare on you then. You'll die slowly, boy, and we'll use a tractor to grind your remains into the earth. No one will ever know. We clear, boy?"

With tears flowing like a river, Cate nodded yes. He was thrown back into the trunk, returned to the church at 1:00 A.M., thrown out onto the hard gravel of the parking lot, and cut loose. He was going to live.

"If you tell any police, if any badge even comes around looking like he's curious, you'll get that final ride, boy," Jenson warned. "No one on this earth will stop me from finding you. You believe that?"

One of the henchmen ripped the duct tape from Cate's mouth, taking a piece of his lip with it.

Bleeding, sobbing, and reeking of gasoline, the broken pastor begged for his life. He told them he would leave first thing. Cole and his men didn't say another word. They just got into the Cadillac and drove away into the night.

Pastor Cate didn't wait for dawn. He packed up everything he owned right then and drove away, still reeking of gasoline. The only thing he left in Belle Glade was a piss stain on the carpet of the Caddy's trunk.

Hickey read the account and some more in the thick report. Closing the cover, he set the report aside and shut his eyes. He still ached. He didn't feel like moving at all. He felt as if he could stay in the bed for a month.

He pulled the covers back and made himself sit up.

When he went to stand, he wobbled, and the plastic line in his arm tugged, calling him to where a sane man would go—back into bed.

Hickey grabbed the tube and yanked it out.

He had work to do now. Work against the Coles. Custer wanted to know where Yoder was, and Hickey was going to make sure they found out, even if he had to personally take on every Cole family member in Belle Glade.

Hickey slowly walked over to the dresser and opened the top drawer. He stared down at the .45 lying atop his running clothes. Fred must have put the gun back where he would find it.

Hickey stripped, redressed in jogging shorts and a T-shirt, and slid into his tennis shoes. He walked out on the beach and began to run. His body rebelled. He fell once and got back up and ran harder then. Hickey willed the pain away and drifted into his runner's form.

He pushed himself along the water's edge by the rhythm of the cadence he sang as he ran. From over thirty years ago, his Fort Bragg Special Forces training kicked in and gave him his orders.

Hickey obeyed.

CHAPTER 15

Each team leader should have a pre-mission and post-mission
checklist to make sure nothing is left behind.

—POI 7658 Special Forces Combat Manual ROV 1970

HICKEY DOVE INTO THE BLUE-GREEN WAVES of the ocean after his run to cool off. He had pushed himself, and he knew he would feel it in the morning. He was feeling it now, but the water soothed him, and swimming evened things out.

He swam out a hundred yards, took a deep breath, and dove straight down. He let the water envelop him as if he were in the womb. Hickey went to the bottom and wormed his fingers and heels into the white sand. He dug in and stayed. The saltwater stung his skin where the IV had been sunk into his arm. He ignored it.

After a minute, his lungs began to complain. Hickey dug into the sand more. After ninety seconds, his lungs started to ache. He let the air bubbles flow out of his mouth. Hickey closed his eyes and tried to go blank in his mind. At two minutes his body told him to escape. Hickey went back to Vietnam. He remembered Larry Yoder lying on that loam of the jungle at midnight before all hell broke loose on that terrible night long ago.

After somewhere between two and a half and three minutes, Hickey brought his hands up above him and, pushing hard with his legs, thrust himself upward toward the sunlight. He broke the surface and took in deep, rewarding breaths of air. He had left the womb.

He lay on his back, floating in the saltwater with his eyes closed, and felt the heat of the Florida sun warm him. He let the current carry him for a few moments before he rolled over and started swimming back for the shore.

The sand of the beach was warm under his feet, and it felt good. He didn't put his running shoes back on but carried them, his T-shirt slung over his shoulder as the water dried on his skin. The sun was blinding, and Hickey felt better.

As he approached Custer's beachfront home, he heard the soft sounds of an old guitar filling the air. He shielded his eyes from the sun and stared onto the porch. Sitting in one of the wooden deck chairs, eyes buried behind wraparound sunglasses, was a man about Hickey's age. He sported a Dallas Cowboys T-shirt, shorts, and some cheap Mexican sandals; his formerly blond hair had grayed, but it was still long and tied back with a thin strip of leather.

Hickey walked under the shaded cover of the deck, stopped, and grinned. The man playing the guitar didn't miss a note and barely moved his stoic eyes to acknowledge Hickey's presence.

"Man, you look old and fucked up," the voice of Dave Hargis intoned, without a trace of humor in his voice. He cocked his head and stared up at his former Special Forces teammate. He stopped playing, dug into his pocket, and came out with a wrinkled dollar bill.

"I didn't know the bums in Florida came up to people's houses." Hargis thrust the dollar out toward Hickey. "Here you go, old man, have a beer on me." He beamed a white-toothed grin at Hickey.

Hickey could do nothing but laugh.

Hargis set his Martin guitar down, stood up, and took his sunglasses off. "How you doing, Hickey?"

Hickey grinned back and thrust his hand out. "Good to see you, Dave."

"What the hell is this? A handshake?" Hargis asked, stepping forward and grabbing Hickey in a bear hug. "Good to see you." They hugged and patted each other's backs.

After that they both settled down onto the deck chairs and started catching up on the thirty-odd years they had been separated.

After Hargis had quit the army, he had headed back to his native Texas. He had landed in Houston. He had been too late for the sixties scene, but there was still plenty of music and lots of clubs around there. He had started playing the small joints like the Jester, where he had become friends with legends like Townes Van Zandt and Lightnin' Hopkins.

Hargis would sit in with them as rhythm guitar. He was also their enforcer and protection when some drunk got out of hand or some club owner just couldn't find any cash to pay the band.

After one club owner had told the three of them that the packed house just hadn't made any money that night, Hargis hadn't hesitated. They were all in the manager's office when Hargis grabbed him by his long, oily hair and slammed his face twice onto the hard wooden desktop.

"What did you say?" Hargis asked the man. "I'm kinda hard of hearing these days."

"My nose!" the club owner screamed, holding his hand up to the bloody, now bent nose.

"Your ears start bleeding next" was all Hargis said, grabbing a pencil from the desktop and calmly staring at the pencil point.

The club owner had suddenly found a fat wad of cash buried deep in his pocket and paid the three men.

Hargis had ended up opening a large live music venue with two other men he had met in Houston. It was called Liberty Hall, and for a decade they brought the best rock and roll, blues, and R&B sounds onto their stage.

He still carried his Smith & Wesson .44 Magnum, with its long, cold, six-inch barrel, under his jacket. He'd only had to pull it once: A young man, shaking from nervousness in his first robbery attempt, had pointed a cheap .25-caliber pistol at the bartender after closing time and demanded cash.

At the time Hargis had been sitting at the end of the bar with the lead singer of the band of the night, a new kid from New Jersey named Bruce Springsteen. Hargis calmly reached under his coat, drew the massive .44, and leveled it at the kid's chest. Then he cocked the hammer.

"You go ahead and shoot him. I was going to fire him soon anyway," Hargis had said calmly.

The shaking kid had heard the hammer cock and turned to see what was there. "So, you shoot, and then I'm going to blow a hole the size of a grapefruit out your back."

Hargis's only worry had been that the kid would accidentally shoot the gun as he started shaking even more. Seeing his chance, the bartender dropped to the floor, and Hargis knew he had a clear shot if need be.

"Now drop that toy and run, you little shit, before you make me waste one of these expensive bullets on your sorry ass."

The Texas-sized embellishment told around the club afterward was that the kid was out the door before his weapon hit the ground.

Hargis and his partners had sold out to some northern investors after the music went where they didn't want to hear it anymore. They had split a tidy profit and gone their separate ways.

After a bout with cocaine and alcohol, Hargis got clean, found a good woman, married her, and they had a beautiful daughter named Jaime. After twenty years, as it often happens, they went their separate ways after their child was off to college. They sold their quaint West University home and split the cash, and Hargis headed back to his native Beaumont. He settled in on two acres with a small house and a big pecan tree under which he sat evenings, plucking away at his songs while smelling the sea breeze and watching the sun drop down.

"And then Fred called me up, and I came here to see what's what," Hargis finished. "I brought my guitar and my toy," Hargis noted, bending down and patting a long black hard case.

"Your toy?" Hickey asked.

"Yep." Hargis smiled. "If you're nice I might let you see her later on."

The screen door opened, and Custer rolled out with a fresh supply of beer for the men on the patio. Right behind him came Jeff Winkler. His hair was still dark and his skin bronzed from spending as much time as he could in his boat—a thirty-foot ski boat.

He had bummed around after the army and ended up in Atlanta. There he started a successful home renovation business and married a soulful woman named Neci, and together they had a daughter named Jackie.

The business had been successful for over fifteen years, and that allowed Winkler the free time to grab his daughter and head out to the lake or deep into the clean North Georgia mountains whenever he wanted. He marveled at his daughter's growth. He found himself spending more and more time with her and leaving the business to his partner and workers as much as he could. There was nothing he wouldn't do for Jackie. Soon enough she would be a teen, and he knew their time together would change.

Hickey was impressed at Winkler's physical bearing. While Hickey ran five miles a day to stay in shape, Winkler's work and time in the mountains kept him lean and tight. He was more than in shape. He kept his tracking skills honed by traveling to the Apache reservations once a year and staying in touch with his roots.

The two old warriors hugged, then sat down and took a beer from the supply on Custer's lap. Custer used the metal frame of his wheelchair to pop the tops.

The four old comrades in arms sat talking and catching up as the Florida sun rose to its zenith. They continued talking out there, enjoying being with each other again, as Geraldine brought a lunch of salad and sandwiches, which they washed down with ice-cold tea.

Custer had already briefed the two newcomers on the situation. They wanted Larry Yoder back, if he was alive; but it was beginning to look as if he had disappeared forever as a result of the Cole family's ruthless methods.

"So, you don't know if he's dead or alive?" Hargis asked, pushing his plate away.

"No idea, Dave, but I intend to find out."

"How many of them are there?" Winkler asked.

"Of the Cole men, at least twenty, between the ages of fifteen and just near seventy. There are only two that old," Custer continued, "Fred and David Cole, the sons of the man who built a sugar empire on blood, fear, and death. And there are at least another thirty men on the Cole payroll as enforcers."

"Layout?" Winkler asked.

"Hickey has been there. He'll tell you what he knows. I am also getting some aerial photo recon pictures of their properties. That's happening today, as a matter of fact."

"I'll go in on foot," Winkler said, "and find out what we need to know."

The table fell into silence.

Before Custer had called the men, he had mailed them the extensive report he had prepared with the intel he had gathered. All the men had read it, and it only brought disgust to their minds.

Custer's men were hard men. They had seen horrible people and events, but little to rival the cold, merciless ways of the Cole family in Belle Glade.

The material read like something from an ugly movie about the Old South and her slaves. Whippings, beatings, rapes, mutilations, and bodies ever disappearing, most likely into the depths of Lake Okeechobee. Little had changed in the seventy years the Coles had held Belle Glade in their iron fists.

The state and county officials were never able to get anything close to court. Their witnesses kept disappearing or fleeing back to their native islands; all of them refused to go near a court in Florida as long as the Coles and their henchmen were around. Even two investigators had disappeared in the Belle Glade vortex over the years. Everyone knew what happened on Cole land, but there was nothing legal that could be done about it.

"So, four against fifty?" Hargis asked.

"Five," Fred corrected. "Dan Hadad arrives later tonight."

"Well, boys, so there's five old troopers against a herd of fifty bad guys," Hargis commented. "Damn, Fred, I thought you said this was going to be a challenge and maybe dangerous." Hargis grinned a Cheshire Cat smile.

"I'd like one more," Hickey spoke up. "A man in England I met on a cross-training exercise. Name's Sharkey. He's tough, a good man. He used to hang out for the queen in Northern Ireland attached to Special Air Service, keeping an eye on the IRA."

The others looked over at Hickey.

"Northern Ireland?" Fred asked. "A man could get killed up there if he's wearing a British uniform."

"Well, Sharkey's retired like us now, and I went on a couple of ops with him. He's solid, and a master with a knife."

"Think he'll go along?" Custer asked.

"If he knows what we know, yes." Hickey didn't hesitate. "He's a man who hates injustice, and inside he's hard. Also, something similar happened to his best friend in Northern Ireland. There is a pub in Poole, England. They'll get a message to him when he comes in. Just ask for Sharkey, his nickname. They'll know him. "

"I'll look into it," Custer said.

Hickey leaned back in his chair. "So, we're all clear here." He looked around the table. "We are going into Belle Glade to try to get Yoder, or his body, back. And if they refuse?" He let the question hang in the humid air.

The question was unnecessary for these men. They had all fought together, and their ties were too deep. That one of their own had possibly been murdered was all they needed to know. Some things run deeper than blood, and laws on paper won't prevent action.

Hargis bent down and lifted his long black hard case, laid it across the chair armrests, and popped the clasps.

"I'm in," Winkler said.

Custer and Hickey were already committed.

Hargis pulled a long, ugly rifle out of the case: It was a custom-made Barrett .50 caliber. He held it up proudly.

"Only fifty against us?" he asked. "Damn, I almost feel sorry for them."

CHAPTER 16

The pack or rucksack can be used as a pillow, however, ensure
that the carrying straps are in the "up" position for easy
insertion of the arms in case of rapid withdrawal.

—POI 7658 Special Forces Combat Manual ROV 1970

DAN HADAD ARRIVED FROM SEATTLE THE next day. After the military, he had gone to Stanford University and gotten an engineering degree. Once he was in the workforce he had discovered computers and dove deep into learning them. By the early eighties he was programming and could write his own ticket wherever he wanted. He had married, settled down, and—like most war veterans—put the war behind him. When the call had come from Custer, he hadn't hesitated; he was on one of Custer's chartered planes the next day. Yoder had saved his life twice in Vietnam, and Hadad was not one to ignore that debt.

After Hadad's arrival, all the men sat around the kitchen table catching up and then running over the intel materials again and again.

Custer had found out through his many contacts where the Brit Sharkey lived, and he let Hickey make the call. Hickey wasn't so stupid as to go over details on an open telephone line, but he and Sharkey had a minor history.

The right hints were dropped and understood across the Atlantic. A quiet man named Van Zandt, whom Custer knew from his Pentagon days, was now retired in Orlando. After Fred called him, he took the next plane from Orlando to Heathrow. Van Zandt was an excellent judge of character, and from long experience he knew Custer's cause was a just one, so he agreed to go without having to be told the details.

From London he took a train to Poole and found the Blue Boar Pub and settled into a booth in the back. He sat away from the crowd, his eyes facing the door. Like many seasoned warriors, he preferred to be able to survey the entire room.

He recognized Sharkey from the photograph Custer had gotten of the man. The quiet man from Orlando didn't know how Custer had acquired the photo, but he wasn't surprised.

Bricklayer—that's what you might think when you saw Sharkey at a pub on a Saturday night. He looked like your average retired bricklayer or dockworker—a bit gone to seed, but who wasn't, these days?

Sharkey was stout, of average height; his gruff-looking face had a scar on the side where he had taken a knife wound decades before. His hairline had receded with the years, but his eyes still shone dark and menacing. Their cold gaze, which when filled with purpose looked like a shark's black eyes, bore down hard and deep, telling you the man behind them was not quitting. That gaze had earned him his nickname in the military.

Out of the corner of Sharkey's eye, that cold gaze caught sight of the quiet man from Orlando and spotted a five-pound note folded like a tent and set up on the end of the table; it was the sign he was looking for. Sharkey took a pint and squeezed into the booth opposite the man Hickey had said would be there.

Though over fifty now, Sharkey still had a hungry look in his eyes.

Neither man was into small talk. After a few words, the stranger from Orlando slid two envelopes across the table. In a large thick one was a copy of Custer's briefing on the Coles. A smaller manila envelope bulged thick with $2,500 in pounds and $2,500 in U.S. dollars.

Van Zandt walked away and was on the last flight out of Heathrow to America. Never wasting a good brew, Sharkey finished his pint before setting off for home. The next day he kissed his wife good-bye, talked to his two hounds—reminding them to be like him and listen to the woman of the house while he was away—and left his quaint cottage. Sharkey was on the first plane he could catch out of Heathrow.

He flew British Airways to Toronto, Canada, where the passport checks remained much less strict than in the United States for a tourist. A perky stewardess named Christine Foye liked his accent and didn't charge him for his drinks. From Toronto, he took a bus to Niagara Falls, New York, on a tourist visa. One of Custer's hired limos picked him up there and took him to a private airport, from which he was flown to Vero Beach.

Both the limo service and airplane charter were owned by former military men to whom Custer had ties. As far as any required paperwork, the British tourist visiting Canada had never been taxied anywhere via their services. Even if anyone had looked for him, he would have seemed to have disappeared into those huge waterfalls in northern New York.

As the five men were sitting around the table in the air-conditioning, three other men were busy at work.

JIM RIGGS, AN O-2 SKYMASTER pilot in Vietnam, and two former Air Force ground crew personnel who had also served there were checking out Riggs's airplane. He had bought a Cessna 337, the civilian version of the O-2, as his dream plane. It had taken him twenty years after leaving the military to save enough to buy it, but now that he had it, he would never want another airplane.

Little known outside the military, the O-2 Skymaster was an air workhorse of the Vietnam War. Also known as "the Duck," the twin-engine military version of the Cessna 337 Super Skymaster airplane was quite a stable platform for those who knew how to fly her. The plane's unusual design had the two engines mounted in tandem, one in front and one in back of the body. This gave the plane what was known as a "push/pull" effect to get it airborne and keep it in the air.

Some had stated that the O-2 had a high accident rate. Most of those who knew the solid craft contended that the failure of pilots to do their proper ground checks before taking off was the problem with most O-2 crashes.

In Vietnam the O-2 was used mostly for ground observation, recon, and laying in phosphorous rockets to the ground. These sent up billowing clouds of white smoke to signal the fast-moving jets coming in to deliver their deadly loads of napalm, five-hundred-pound bombs, or 20 mm cannon rounds.

While anyplace in a war zone could be dangerous, there were far more risky occupations than flying the slow-moving O-2s. The plane was generally flown at 155 to 170 knots as it coasted high above the jungle canopy between 1,500 and 2,000 feet. This was far enough above the jungle that ground fire shot upward was ineffective. The main antiaircraft weapon of the North Vietnamese was the Russian SAM missile. There was no way that the North Vietnamese manning those missiles were going to shoot a million-dollar weapon at a fifty-thousand-dollar American plane. Those shots were saved for the expensive jets and B-52 bombers.

Regionally based by the army and air force in Vietnam, the O-2 pilots relied on flying over the same ground, again and again, until they could spot any differences in the terrain. The pilots would investigate these. They would also photograph them, call in serious ordnance, or assist the U.S. ground troops as they could.

After the war, Riggs had kept up his private license, and he still loved taking wing anytime he could. He was more than happy to keep his license current by flying halfway across the country to Florida when Custer contacted him. They had known each other in the Kontum district, from which Custer's Special Forces team had operated. Riggs had been stationed there to fly his O-2 during the same period. As he had with so many others, Custer had maintained contact with Riggs over the years.

Riggs was never told why Custer, the former Special Forces soldier, wanted complete overhead photos of a place called Belle Glade. He figured the man was working on another investment. Since Custer was paying all expenses, Riggs was happy to do the job.

Riggs looked up on the Internet the private Orlando airport that Custer suggested, and then he got all the maps he would need for the trip. Custer had suggested Orlando because of the huge number of tourists flowing in and out of the mega-theme-parked land that Mickey Mouse built. With Orlando taking in millions of visitors from all over the globe every year, what was one more tourist coming in?

After he landed there, Riggs turned his O-2 over to the two men who owned the airport. Riggs called a cab, took it to a local hotel, and rested a couple of days, giving the men time to do their work.

Don Whitmir and Hill DeWolf were solid ground crew men, well trained in many different aircraft after thirty years each in the air force. Both had retired around 1990, but they wanted to remain around planes. Running a private airport in the land of Disney was profitable enough, and they added to that business by doing the routine engine work any properly maintained aircraft needs.

Both men's wives swore that the men spent more time together with the airplanes than they did with them. To those who didn't know them, the pair often appeared to fight. After nearly fifteen years together on their little piece of Orlando, they had arguments over which wrench to use or what brand of oil was best for which engine. These apparent arguments were really window dressing: They were, in fact, detailed, technical discussions. The two men worked well together, and Riggs was paying cash for a complete check. They had the plane ready by seven the morning that he came to take his flight over Belle Glade.

Whitmir and DeWolf waved him off after his thirty-minute preflight check and watched him take to the air in his unique O-2. Whitmir hadn't worked on one since he was stationed in Vietnam. The plane had brought back fond memories as he poked around under the engine cowling.

After Riggs was at two thousand feet and heading south, he opened the flight bag at his side and pulled out a Nikon F6 35 mm film camera and a Canon EOS-1Ds Mark III digital camera. Custer had had these delivered to Riggs in his hotel room by the quiet Orlando man. Riggs had used a Nikon F6 numerous times, but it took him a few hours to get familiar with the new Canon while waiting in the room. It impressed him, and he thought he might have to get one for himself.

Since Belle Glade was only a hundred air miles from Orlando, Riggs knew he would have no problem with fuel. He noted how his beloved Skymaster trimmed out well and handled better than before. He attributed this to the two retired mechanics as he watched Florida's vistas flow beneath his plane.

He took his altitude down to a thousand feet as he crossed the top edge of Lake Okeechobee. After locating Belle Glade, he started taking pictures, switching between cameras. Custer had marked a map with areas in which he was interested, and after two passes Riggs had what he needed. He took the plane farther south and landed in Miami to refuel. As the pump topped his tank off, he reloaded the massive Nikon bulk film pack, which allowed 250 shots before having to be loaded again.

As Custer had suggested, Riggs killed a couple of hours on the ground and then took off north again. His third pass over Belle Glade was at five hundred feet, and he used every frame of film in the Nikon and filled up another Canon 8 GB memory card with images of the fields and buildings around there. No one on the ground noticed the little airplane floating past Belle Glade on its passes south and then later north.

By 2:00 P.M., he was back in Orlando and calling Custer from a throwaway cell phone Custer had bought just for this part of the operation. He didn't know it, but the other cell phone he called from was never used again. It ended up destroyed in Custer's garage, the pieces thrown away in a public wastebasket near the beach.

The quiet man who had delivered the equipment the day before came for the film, memory cards, and cell phone within an hour. Riggs handed them over and tried to do the same with the cameras, but the man refused those. Riggs was handed their original boxes, manuals, and everything else, plus an envelope with five thousand dollars in cash. The next Christmas he would receive the usual Christmas card from Custer and Geraldine, with a short note stating, "Thanks for your help."

Riggs didn't know what prompted such expensive gifts as an eight-thousand-dollar Canon camera and a nice stack of greenbacks, and he never asked. Like almost everyone who ever met Custer, Riggs respected him and never spoke of what he did for the man. If Fred Custer was behind it, there was a good reason for it.

By 7:00 P.M. the film had been developed and every film and digital image had been printed as an eight-by-ten-inch photo. It had taken four employees at Orlando's best photo lab to finish the work, and all had stayed past the usual 5:00 P.M. closing time. The owner was paying triple time, cash, for the rush job, and his bill to the man in a wheelchair in Vero Beach was triple that.

Van Zandt had everything at Custer's doorstep by 10:00 P.M. and was back home in Orlando by midnight. He owed Custer from his Pentagon days, and he was more than happy to forget everything he did while repaying the debt.

The five former Special Forces comrades started poring over the pictures after a late dinner. They stayed up until 1:00 A.M., deciding which pictures gave them the information they needed to plan and continue their operation.

Custer warned them that they had all better get some sleep, because tomorrow, after they picked up Sharkey, he was going to take them to Tampa and have fun with them.

Questions were asked about what he meant.

Fred Custer kept a poker face and told them that they would see for themselves.

CHAPTER 17

Team work, the key to success, only comes through
constant practice and training.

—POI 7658 Special Forces Combat Manual ROV 1970

THE SIX FORMER SPECIAL FORCES TROOPERS groaned, complained, and knew they would be feeling the pains of being fifty and not twenty-one anymore. They kept doing what they were told anyway.

After picking up the gregarious Sharkey, they settled into the large van and hit the road across Florida. They wondered where Custer was taking them, but he still wasn't talking.

Custer had borrowed the van with the three bench seats in the back from a friend who ran tourists up to Cape Canaveral during the season. As they rolled across Florida toward the Gulf of Mexico, they got to know the strange Englishman who was now with them. Only Hickey knew Sharkey, and as the two old troopers spoke of training and of field operations together, the others took the measure of the bearlike man, who sported an out-of-style handlebar mustache but pulled that off.

Men who have seen combat, especially former Special Forces troopers, can quickly discern the truth behind the words of a man who speaks of operations where bullets have flown. Sharkey was not boasting with his stories of his days in Northern Ireland, hiding in bushes or hedges for hours at a time spying on the IRA. He just told it as it was.

Although Sharkey liked adding humor into his tales when he could, the true bloody nature of his military days in that place where no British citizen is ever truly welcome spoke enough to those around him. British soldiers were automatically marked for death by the IRA in those days.

By the time they reached Tampa, Sharkey was one of the team.

In Tampa, they got the answer to the question of where they were going. It was in the form of a dojo owned by 7th Dan Master Jeff Cope. Cope might have been approaching fifty, but he didn't look it. Always a natural athlete, a college baseball player who just couldn't hit quite enough fastballs to make the pros, Cope had attacked golf, fishing, hunting, and anything else outdoors from his twenties to his forties. Then he had discovered Hap Ki Do.

Little known in America except by serious martial arts students, Hap Ki Do was born on February 21, 1948, at a Korean brewery. Forty-four-year old Yong Sul Choi was working to earn some grain to feed his pigs by pumping water for the brewery. Some men tried to force him off his pump. He defended himself.

Bok Sop Suh, the son of the owner of the brewery, saw the fight through his office window. He was impressed by the man's fighting style and the ease with which he dispatched his opponents. The young Bok Sop Suh went down to the stranger pumping water and asked him to train him. Choi agreed. The payment was in cash and grain, and Hap Ki Do was officially born. Before he left this world, Grandmaster Choi had made his mark.

Hap Ki Do is close in attitude to the Japanese Aikido: Both forms use joint locks or attacks, pressure, or the breaking of bones to achieve their goals. Only Ed Parker's purely American Kenpo—generally lacking the Oriental mental aspects of the martial arts—and Bruce Lee's Jeet Kune Do are as fast and bone-breaking. Of these four forms, only Aikido seriously lends itself to tournament competition. The others are too brutal in action to use fully against others unless in sincere combat.

Jeff Cope found that he loved the study of Hap Ki Do. He excelled at it and earned his black belt with four years of hard work. His successful real estate business allowed him the time to schedule his long training sessions, and soon he felt physically better then he ever had before in his life.

When the dojo at which he studied was threatening to close for lack of students, Cope used his real estate connections to find an old warehouse in Tampa. The two buildings had been seized in a drug raid, and when they came to auction, he was there to bid. No investors were seriously interested because, for development purposes, the location was all wrong. It was on the far edge of the city, and there was no infrastructure around it. Cope won the property for a fraction of its market value.

The dojo was moved to its new home, three times the size of the former location. Always a savvy businessman, Cope was able to rent out one building to more than pay the taxes. He knew one day that ever growing Tampa would drive the value of his buildings well past a million, but that would be at least a decade away; for now, he had a place to train and to help train others.

Cope knew Custer from when Fred and Geraldine were fishing the Gulf for tarpon. For whatever reason, destiny or luck, they had ended up on the same private charter boat. Sharing fishing lines and cigars, the two men had hit it off. Ever since then, Custer would drive over three times a year and put himself through a weeklong session of physical training and toning.

Cope was at first apprehensive about training the mild-looking man in a wheelchair, but after Fred used the side of the chair to pull a surprised Cope off balance—a difficult thing to do—and threw him to the mat, Jeff Cope started taking the man seriously.

As he lay on his own mat, staring up at Custer, he was asked a question.

"What will you do now?" Fred Custer smiled down.

Cope trained the man as hard as any of his other students, and Fred pushed himself once again past where most thought he could go.

When Custer called asking if he could rent the entire dojo for seven days for a group of men who needed to be put into shape, Cope didn't want to do it. This would mean no other classes, especially at night. The nights were when the now lucrative kid and teen classes filled the dojo. Jeff Cope deeply enjoyed teaching the kids.

Fred mentioned a cash price that delayed the lessons of others for seven days.

When the six men arrived, Cope was ready. Custer had told him these were all men who could be pushed, and by God he wanted them pushed. Cope saw determination within the eyes of all the men, and he went to work on them.

For seven long days he prodded, pushed, commanded, and instructed them. He made them work until they groaned. Even the two fittest of the men—Hickey and Winkler—were surprised by the new aches they got for their efforts.

Cope watched each morning, before his first session with the men, as Custer took off in a rented golf cart with the men jogging behind him to the beach and back. The beach was three miles away, across the back roads and bike trails Custer had scouted out so he could use the golf cart.

The first morning they did this, the men thought the run to the beach was hard enough. As they heard the waves crashing against the beach, they wondered what the little green pile was in front of them.

Always a champion in training and operation execution, Custer had let them run to the beach thinking that was the hard part. The five men didn't smile when they saw the Alice packs waiting there on the beach. Custer had surprised them again: Each green military backpack was weighed down with forty pounds of rocks, and no one liked the idea of running back with those monsters dragging him down.

To their credit, not one of them complained.

"Well," Hickey spoke out, as he hefted the pack on his back and tightened the straps around his shoulders and waist, "at least he got the small Alice packs and not the big ones."

Custer watched as, just as he had thought it would, the jog back became a competition between the former soldiers. They teased and prodded each other onward. They sang old running-cadence songs from Fort Bragg, and Sharkey taught them some new ones from England. They were laughing when they reached Cope's dojo again.

After resting, they began their training under Master Cope. Lunch was light and quick before they started an afternoon session and then another full-pack run to the beach and back.

Cope had no idea what was up, but he knew better than to ask.

That night at the hotel, they soaked in the hot, swirling waters of the outdoor Jacuzzi. Then they plunged into the cold pool water. Physically worn out, they were all asleep by 10:00 P.M. and back up at dawn to do it all over again.

By the end of those seven days, they were physically tougher and trained in some minor Hap Ki Do techniques, and the loaded Alice packs were almost not hated. More important, they were coming together as a team.

They said good-bye to Master Cope and thought they would

be heading back to Vero Beach, but Custer had yet another surprise for them. They drove south now, down toward Naples. Stopping well above it, they got off the busy Interstate 75 and onto a two-lane road and then a long, bumpy dirt road deep into the heart of the Florida swamp lands.

Custer had found a large tract of land owned by a German he knew. The man came to Florida only during the winter. One day he would move here, but for now this land was his investment and not used for anything. The closest town was twenty miles away and the closest neighbors ten. It was perfect for what they needed now.

The silent man from Orlando had arrived and set up a rifle range on the land while the men trained in Tampa. There were twenty-five- and fifty-yard targets for the pistols and one-hundred-, five-hundred-, and thousand-yard targets for the rifles. After the van stopped and all the men were out, Custer pointed at the long wooden boxes in front of them, and these were pried open.

Inside were brand-new military M-16s, AK-47s, some of the fine H&K 9 mm MP5s, Colt .45 and Beretta 9 mm pistols, and even six deadly claymores. Winkler found one of his favorite 5.56 mm Stoner rifles.

There was enough ammo for all of the guns to end a third world coup.

Everyone was quiet, wondering where their former Vietnam leader had acquired these fully automatic, fully military weapons. If there was any question in their minds before, it was now answered. There was nothing legal about anything they were looking at.

"Fred," Dan Hadad opened up, "these aren't exactly Wal-Mart items."

"Well, Dan," Fred responded, "we aren't on a dove hunting trip, are we?"

"Where did you get all of these?" Sharkey asked. As a British citizen, he was surprised by the massive collection of firepower before him.

"Let's just say in Miami, cash goes a long way if you know the right people," Fred responded. "No questions asked. They even deliver."

"Bloody hell," came the response. "You Yanks. It's like the Wild West."

They all laughed.

"We'll make a lot of noise out here," Hickey noted.

"And we'll only be scaring alligators," Custer stated. "No one for miles around."

Hargis spotted his long black case and walked over and opened it up. He carefully pulled out his sleek, deadly .50-caliber rifle, loaded a clip, walked over, and lay down in front of the thousand-yard targets.

Not one of the others had ever seen one of these weapons in action before, and they came over to watch. Custer dug out some field glasses and wheeled himself over to spot for the Texan.

The .50-caliber had been a devastating machine-gun round before it was first developed as a sniper weapon by a bored army sniper in the early seventies. The half-inch-wide, two-inch-long round could rip through almost anything found on the battlefield. Since 1921, it had been used on airplanes, tanks, and ships at sea. It had been used by ground troops all over the globe.

Ronnie Barrett, a former law enforcement officer and long-range shooting enthusiast, had started Barrett Firearms Manufacturing in Murfreesboro, Tennessee, in 1982 to supply weapons to army snipers. Barrett made the finest .50-caliber military rifles available, and that same basic design was still sold on the civilian market as the Model 82A1 at a cost of around eight thousand dollars.

The rifle weighed a little more than thirty pounds. Its twenty-nine-inch barrel could send one of the rounds flying out with a muzzle velocity of more than 2,900 feet per second and deliver up to 11,500 foot-pounds of energy upon impact. Although the clip could hold up to ten rounds, no experienced sniper would load more than nine. According to U.S. Army official statistics, a ball or armor-piercing round could travel over eight thousand yards, more than four miles. And with the Barrett's unique recoil system, it felt like the shooter was firing only a 12-gauge shotgun at his shoulder.

While that four-mile distance was impossible for any sniper to work at effectively, the weapon could easily deliver deadly firepower up to a mile. At up to two thousand yards a trained shooter could put rounds through brick walls, most vehicles, bulletproof vests, or just about anything else under the scope hairs.

At 656 yards, one of the deadly bullets could punch through a half inch of face-hardened armor plate, twelve inches of sand, twenty-seven inches of clay, or one inch of concrete. Its effects on the human body were documented and devastating.

David Hargis had been shooting his massive rifle for years now and could easily deliver the bullets on target.

Everyone was silent as Hargis relaxed on the ground and positioned his body behind the weapon. From their own rifle experience, the men knew when Hargis had found the paper target a thousand yards away; they watched as he let out half of a deep breath, waiting to squeeze the trigger.

The sound was massive as he let go the first round.

"Two inches left," Custer barked out.

"Humidity" was Hargis's only response. He readjusted, took another breath, and squeezed off a second round.

"Bull's-eye!" Custer stated.

Hargis didn't say another word, but he let the rifle talk, sending four more rounds into the target. Custer yelled, "Bull's-eye!" after each shot.

After that, all the men wanted a chance to try the new weapon. They were all surprised by the weapon's ease of use and lack of recoil. None of them could even come close to Hargis's accuracy, though.

They broke out the other rifles and pistols and checked them out. They all loaded clips and emptied the rounds into the targets.

Then they fieldstripped the weapons and cleaned and oiled them, finding that the illegal gun sellers had given Custer good value for his money.

More ammo boxes were broken open, and clips were refilled round by gleaming round. Dusk was taking over by then. It was Dan Hadad, ever the thinking-ahead engineer, who looked around and noticed no house or building on the German's land.

"Where are we sleeping?" he asked, sliding round after round into AK clips.

"I was wondering when I was going to get asked about that," Custer mused. "Open that," he said, pointing to the largest wooden box.

Hargis and Hickey grabbed a crowbar and pried the nails out of the top of a big crate. It was filled with two large Army surplus tents, six sleeping bags, and MREs. The MREs, officially labeled "Meals, Ready to Eat" by the military, were full meals of various foods, on disposable plates, sealed in green, brown, or white plastic bags. They were the main food of the United States Army and Marines while in the field. Each package was labeled "U.S. Government Property. Commercial Resale Is Unlawful." Men loading illegal fully automatic weapons could hardly be expected to take such a warning seriously.

Like every other primary field food of every military force in the history of the world, MREs were generally loathed by men who had to eat them. They had earned such nicknames as "Meals Rejected by Everyone," "Meals Rejected by the Enemy," or "Mr. E," referring to their mysterious texture and taste. There were other names, far from complimentary, given to these packages by those who had eaten them.

"Couldn't find C-rats?" Hargis joked, referring to the little green metal cans of various foods that were the mainstay of the military ground forces during the Vietnam War.

But food is food when one is in the field. The tents were pitched, sleeping bags unrolled, wood gathered, and a fire started.

They set up camp. Once again, Fred Custer was dragging the men back to their military ways. Being solid Special Forces men, they all fell in line.

Under the last of the camping goods, the crate floor was covered with bottled water and one case of Miller beer. Although the beer was warm and nothing fancy, it was generally welcomed by the men after their meal. Only Sharkey refused the American brew after tasting one.

"How can you drink this swill?" he asked, digging into the pack he had toted.

He produced an old, battered tin cup, added water, and set it to heat over the fire. When the water was boiling, he wrapped his hand in an old rag, grabbed the tin, and added some good British tea. Like most British soldiers, no matter where they were in the world, he never traveled without his tea.

Sharkey had made one special weapon request of Custer and had happily pulled an old U.S. Marine K-bar knife from the pile of weapons. He started running the cold steel back and forth across a whetstone, bringing the knife to a razor-sharp edge in between sips of tea.

"Sharkey's a knife man," Hickey noted.

"Damn right," the Brit added.

"K-bar, eh?" Hargis asked.

"Best combat knife I have ever found," Sharkey noted. "If I can't conk 'em over the head with the butt, I use the business end."

Firing any weapon in a war zone—and Northern Ireland was that when he was stationed there—would just give your position away, and someone might fire back. A knife was silent and quite effective for those trained in its proper use.

Hargis pulled out his guitar and started to play as each man had his ration of two beers. Night enveloped them, and the stars filled the sky. The crickets chirped, and fireflies lit up at the edge of the trees around them.

As such men are apt to do, they talked of battles won and lost, of wives or girlfriends also won or lost; and then the subject of Larry Yoder came up.

"Sharkey, we know why we're all here, but why are you here?" Custer asked.

The Brit stopped sharpening his blade and looked up through the firelight.

"Because of Colin Bohanna," Sharkey stated. "He was more than a mate to me. More like a brother. Better than any brother I had."

He was silent and went back to scraping the blade slowly across the stone, the noise the only sound in the camp.

"He was grabbed by the IRA." The sound of the blade on stone grew a bit louder. "We knew some of their hiding spots. Every unit searched for him."

The sound of the steel on stone was now constant in tempo and tone.

"We found him, all right. But not in time." Sharkey turned, looking each man, one by one, in the eyes. "We figured it took him two days to die. Wasn't a pretty sight, mind you. Closed-casket funeral."

Sharkey slowly pulled the blade up and examined the edge, satisfied.

"He and my sister were to be wed a fortnight later. Broke her heart." He slid the knife into its leather scabbard. "So I'm paying back a debt."

The camp lapsed into silence after that.

After a while, the sound of a map being unfolded broke the silence. Winkler had unfolded a Florida road map. He handed it over to Custer.

"Where are we now?" he asked his commander.

"Here." Custer brought his finger down onto the paper on the opposite side of Lake Okeechobee from Belle Glade.

"I want to scout where we'll be," Jeff said.

"No problem. We can drive through on the way back and drop you off."

"Do you have a map of the town?" Jeff asked.

Custer pulled out a canvas field shoulder case and pulled the flap back. He rooted around, coming up with a thick Rand McNally spiral-bound map of Palm Beach County, including Belle Glade, and then a thin, folded map of the city itself. He thrust them toward the quiet tracker.

Wordlessly, Winkler walked back to his spot around the fire and started studying the maps.

"What's the plan, Colonel?" Hickey asked.

"We give them one more chance to do things quiet and nice," Custer replied. "Then we go in loaded for bear."

"We have no idea of Yoder's status? Alive? Forced away like the other man? Dead?" Hadad asked.

"Nothing confirmed, but I fear the worst," Custer replied. "If he was on the run . . . well, he wouldn't be, but if that had happened, I would have heard from him. He is either being held captive somewhere or he was murdered. Our job is to find out which."

"I'll keep hope open, but after my experience, I don't see much chance of him being alive. I was lucky to escape alive. They sure wanted me dead," Hickey noted.

"Then we get the body," Custer stated flatly.

"Yes, sir," Hickey replied.

"I don't need this," Winkler stated, handing the large spiral-bound map back to Custer. "How many days here?"

"Three, or maybe four," Custer said.

"I'd like to be dropped off around there on a Friday afternoon."

"Three full days here, then. We'll leave Friday morning," Fred said.

With decisions made and plans in place, they talked a while more and, one by one, drifted off to sleep.

FOR THREE FULL DAYS THEY fired weapons, ran teams against each other in the woods, jogged, and practiced live-fire escape and evasion maneuvers through the heavy woods and on the edge of the swamps. At night they rested under the stars, the hard ground their beds, reminding all of younger men in faraway places.

The night before they left, Winkler said nothing as he slipped into the woods. In fact, no one heard him slip away. Only when he returned, firmly holding a two-foot alligator in his hands, did anyone know he had gone anywhere.

"Found him in the water," he said, holding forth the animal. "Always wanted to see one up close. I had to outrun the mother."

"You outran a gator?" Hargis asked, then noted, "Some of them can run thirty miles per hour on land."

"But not sideways," Winkler added. "They can't run for shit sideways."

"Classic E&E, Winkler," Hadad noted.

Winkler had bound the reptile's jaws with a leather strip he carried, winding it numerous times around the gator's mouth, then tying it off in a knot. He passed the reptile around from man to man. When they had all examined the little gator, Winkler spoke again.

"I'll take it back now." Then he was gone again like a ghost into the night.

THE NEXT MORNING THEY LOADED the guns and other equipment back into the wooden crates. Carefully, they policed up any trace that they had been there. The worst part was picking up the hundreds of spent brass cartridges they had fired off, but they got them all.

By 11:00 A.M., they were again on the rutted back road, and by noon on Highway 27, just below Venus, running south. That soon took them to Highway 80, which cut across Florida parallel to the more famous "Alligator Alley" connecting Naples, on the Gulf, to Miami, on the Atlantic. They stopped in Clewiston and filled up with gas and had their first meal at a table in four days.

Fred Custer used another disposable cell phone and called Van Zandt in Orlando to pick up the boxes from the desolate land on which they had trained. The weapons were placed in a North Palm Beach storage facility; Custer had one of the two keys to the padlock. When they were ready, they could grab the weapons without having to see another human being.

Sharkey took Custer's cell phone into the bathroom. He pulled the battery and pocketed it. Then he used a pocket knife to pry the phone apart and destroyed the guts. Those went into his other front pants pocket.

The battery was disposed of in the gas station trash. The rest of the phone went down an embankment and into the lake when they made a quick stop on the road. With that done, they headed into Belle Glade a few miles ahead.

Only Custer and Hickey had seen the town before. As they passed the tin shacks on the lakeside, where the poorest cane harvesters lived, they could only marvel at the squalor.

"It's like the bloody third world," Sharkey commented.

They felt sure that no one would recognize "Mr. Devlin" in the van, but Hickey ducked low just the same, lying down on the backseat. To anyone looking, the van was just another gang of tourists going somewhere.

As they rolled into Belle Glade proper, Winkler pointed to the same Texaco where Hickey had met the county officer many nights before.

"This is good," he said. "Flashlight. Pen."

Sharkey passed him a small LED flashlight. Custer produced a red wax pencil that he used to mark maps and handed that over to Winkler.

Winkler slipped out of the van, turned to the men, and said, "I'll see you in two days." And he was away.

They drove through the town twice, with Custer pointing out areas of interest to them all.

Cutting up Main Street, they went north until they hit the small private airport. They went east on Airport Boulevard until they found West Sugar House Road. Going north again, they were soon surrounded by the sugarcane fields. Soon they passed a large house looming a quarter mile off the road.

"That's Fred Cole's home," Custer pointed out.

When they passed a second large, plantation-style home, he noted, "And that's David Cole's house."

"Sugar pays pretty well," Sharkey commented.

"For some," Hickey piped up, from his position lying across the last bench seat.

At Curlee Road they cut back west, catching Main Street again, then drove south, back toward town. At Airport Boulevard they turned east again but ignored the cutoff toward the Coles' homes and instead continued straight ahead. Farther down the road, they found Duda Road and went north again.

Off this road, surrounded by the acres of cane, were a couple of other buildings the Coles owned.

"Those are their warehouses and storage facilities," Custer noted.

Hickey rose to a sitting position now that they were out of Belle Glade proper. Another house appeared off the road, an average ranch-style home.

"Fred's son, Jenson Cole, lives there, closest to the facilities," Custer said.

They all looked quietly at the buildings and wondered what would happen. The road hit Highway 80/441. They took that east, building up speed with the other cars on the road, and headed to the busy Interstate 95, which took them back to Vero Beach.

CHAPTER 18

If followed by trackers, change direction of movement
often and attempt to evade or ambush your trackers.
They make good PWs.

—POI 7658 Special Forces Combat Manual ROV 1970

W INKLER WALKED INTO THE COOL AIR-CONDI-
tioning of the Texaco store. Like anyone unused to South
Florida's hot July temperatures, he was surprised by the sudden
chilling air-conditioning, which battled the humidity outside.
Having spent time in the desert, he was used to heat, but this was
different.

He found what he needed on the shelves stocked with goods
for tourists. A black backpack with MY FOLKS WENT TO FLORIDA
AND ALL I GOT WAS THIS would suit his needs. To that he added
two bottles of Fiji bottled water, a roll of electrical tape, a small
notebook of blank paper, a dozen Met-Rx energy bars, another

flashlight, extra batteries, and two bottles of Gatorade. Finally, he bought one bottle of cheap wine.

He could easily live off the land anywhere in the world if it could be lived off. After leaving Vietnam and the military, Winkler had spent some time in the southern Arizona reservations of Grandfather's Apache tribes. He walked into the worst part of the hard wasteland deserts for a month with nothing but a knife and a gallon of water. A young tribe member, also a scout, told him he was crazy to go off into that desert with so little.

"You're going to die," the man had warned.

"Be here in a month" was all Winkler had said back.

Those desolate lands along the Mexican border could not be survived by the unprepared for more than a few days. Hundreds of Mexicans crossing the border each year perished in that place for lack of knowledge of how to live off nature. The Apaches generally felt there was no way a white man could survive out there. There were bets on whether the strange white man would return.

With years of training and experience, however, Winkler had had no problems finding food and water. When the month was up, the young Apache was waiting in an old Chevy pickup truck. As Winkler opened the door and sat down, the old seat springs sagging under his weight, the driver looked over.

"Well?" he questioned. "How was it?"

"Nice. Quiet" was the stoic reply.

He could easily get by without the things he had bought at the Texaco store, but he saw no point in doing that. Gathering food took time in the field, and he wanted that time to scout the land.

He also had a message to deliver. He and Custer had discussed it after Winkler said he wanted to see the land. He was to provide a final chance for the corrupt Cole family to tell them where Larry Yoder was, and his physical state.

The Coles would be told again that no questions would be asked if that information was given freely. There would be no investigations, no repercussions. The Coles would have a chance to walk away free from any problems as far as Custer and his men were concerned; but one way or another, they would get that information.

After paying for the goods, Winkler headed into the bathroom and locked the door. First, he slid an eight-inch knife and scabbard from where it had been in the small of his back. He placed this into the base of the backpack. Next came the drinks and energy bars, the wine, and then the extra batteries. He zipped the main compartment closed.

He then unwrapped the electrical tape and placed strips across most of the flashlight lenses. He shut the bathroom light off and tested the lights. With the tape covering the lenses, they barely sent out a small shaft of light. It was enough. He would use the LED mostly to mark the map, not to see by. He turned the bathroom lights back on.

The two flashlights and electrical tape went into a smaller zippered compartment on the backpack. Finally the map, notebook, and red wax pen went into the top, mesh-pocketed section.

Winkler slipped out of the bathroom and the Texaco station unnoticed; just another tourist, or maybe one of the cane workers. He headed off down SW Avenue E to explore the town of Belle Glade.

HE WALKED ALL AFTERNOON UNNOTICED as he explored. He saw the ragged, run-down apartment buildings crammed full of the poor immigrants who each year grew and then cut the cane. He saw the barely better-off lower-middle-class homes of the families who had been born here but never managed to escape.

The homes, restaurants, and bars of those who supervised the work did not impress him. He had seen better elsewhere. It was a small town, and it had the establishments a small town usually has.

Near dusk, he stared out from the edge of the golf course into the trees around it. Winkler had never understood golf courses— they were an incredible waste of nature's gifts, an insult to the

Spirit Who Moves Through All. Suddenly, Winkler heard men approaching. Crouching down into the tall grasses, he watched and listened, as still as an untouched pond.

It was a foursome playing golf. When one of the men's golf balls landed not five feet away from him in the grass, he heard it fall. He made no motion, no sound. When the fat man bounded over, huffing and puffing, to find the lost ball, he never noticed the silent tracker less than two yards from him. He went back to his game after throwing his ball back onto the fairway.

When the men had moved on, Winkler headed for the lake. He found a good camping spot and caught a fish for dinner. He made sure his spot was away from any eyes as he lit a fire, gutted the fish, then cooked it on a stick. He washed it down with Gatorade to return the lost salts he had sweated out all day.

Putting the backpack back on, he then set out to explore the lake's edge. He walked almost back to Highway 80 before he found some campsites of the truly destitute. He made himself known and found three Jamaican men who spoke English well enough.

It wasn't so much that they welcomed strangers to their camps—they were generally leery—but the unopened bottle of wine Winkler held out in his left hand bought him a spot around the fire.

Pretending to be a vagrant on the road looking for work, he asked them about the conditions of working around Belle Glade. He didn't mention the Coles. He didn't have to. He was told all about that family and their harsh ways.

Two of the men showed him scars, and one told him of a friend who had crossed a supervisor. That man had disappeared a few days later and was never heard from again. Winkler was told all this and more. Things weren't as bad as Custer's data said: They were worse.

There were words about an annual get-together of the Cole men and their white supervisors out at the main warehouse. This party was held during the Labor Day holiday. Booze and cocaine were trucked in from Miami, porno films were shown on a big-screen TV, and the men partied until they were ready for some women.

No women were invited to this gathering, but some were taken there. The wives or daughters of workers on the shit list were forcibly taken to the warehouse and kept locked behind tin doors, where they had to listen to the men's party get more and more boisterous. By midnight the men were high and ready, and then the women were dragged out and used.

It was a tradition that any sixteen-year-old Cole boy lost his virginity at those gatherings. Drunk, usually not for the first time, he would take one of the women on a hard wooden table in front of all. The table had little other use, and no one knew how many women had been raped there.

As the Jamaicans passed the bottle, with Winkler barely drinking, he took all of this in. When he had heard enough, he thanked the men, left the wine for them, walked off into the darkness, and made his way back to his campsite. He lay back but couldn't fall asleep until long past midnight. Little bothered him these days, but what he had heard did.

Winkler woke in the morning to the sounds of something moving through the thick brush close to the lake where he had bedded. He didn't move, but let his ears explore the sounds; his hand silently went to the handle of the knife he had placed at his side before falling asleep. He had heard the noises before. They were not man-made. They were far too eloquent for most men in the outdoors.

It was a doe and her fawn cautiously nosing their way through the brush and reeds to the lake's edge. Winkler knew that the mother was teaching her fawn how to glide along the thick cover to drink safely from the lake.

He knew he could easily kill the doe for her meat by stalking her and using his knife. He rarely used a rifle or pistol when hunting. That was no challenge and didn't keep his skills sharp. There was no point to hunting the deer. He didn't need the food, and killing the doe would doom the fawn to an early death.

He had never killed for sport and, like many hunters, had left his days of killing game behind him unless for survival. He still stalked game, but just for the thrill of seeing nature's animals in their own environments.

He rose slowly and crept silently toward the sounds of the deer lapping water. The fawn would be less knowledgeable of natural predators at its age, but the mother would be fully alert, guarding her child. This was a good challenge.

He closed his eyes and felt the slight breeze on his face. He was downwind of the deer, so he wouldn't have to circle above them. Like a snake gliding through the brush, he was beyond silent, with over forty years of tracking and stalking skills behind him.

Soon his face was barely poking through some reeds just three yards from the deer.

He froze like granite and watched as the mother and child took their fill of the lake's cool water. The doe's eyes even passed over him twice without seeing him. Winkler knew that deer do not have good eyesight; they depend on their ears more than on their eyes.

He waited until they were finished and had slipped back into the deep brush around the lake before he went into the cold water and bathed.

He spent the rest of that day slowly circling Belle Glade in an expanding circle. He ran the black earth of the cane fields through his fingers, smelling it, even tasting the earth.

By the afternoon he had seen most of the town and many of the fields around it. He settled in, watching the Coles' large warehouse from the edge of one cane field. He saw nothing unexpected; an occasional truck pulled up, and bags were unloaded and stored. After watching without moving for close to two hours, he saw his opportunity: Winkler got the chance he had been waiting for.

The truck that pulled up around four o'clock was loaded with some bags, and the only two men around the warehouse drove off, leaving the building doors open. He knew that the men would be back to lock up, but right now the tin building was his to explore.

Quickly, Winkler moved into the hot tin-roofed warehouse. It was mainly a large open space with pallets of fertilizer and other farming goods stacked against the walls. Sitting against the wall farthest from the wide-open doors was a long wooden table. He now knew what that was used for.

Three large industrial fans were built into the back wall. They were off now, but when spinning, they would cut the wicked heat of South Florida to tolerable levels. There was also a regular back door in the middle of the wall under the fans.

There was one small storage room added onto each side of the building. Each was fifteen by ten feet and made of the same tin material as the rest of the building; each had a plain wooden door with a padlock hasp screwed into the frame and door. The door on the far side from Winkler was open, with an open padlock hanging from the rusty hasp. That was where the women were kept, locked up while the Coles and their men partied.

The other room was locked, but it didn't take much effort for Winkler to climb the wall and look down into the unroofed room. Here were the guns of the Cole family. The walls of the little room had wooden racks with pump shotguns, deer rifles, and a handful of pistols all lined up. If he had had the small hand tools and the time, Winkler would have dropped down and removed the firing pins from the weapons, but he didn't know when the men would be back.

He settled for drawing the floor plan onto the blank notebook pages and slipping back into the surrounding cane fields. It was dusk, time to move on and to deliver the final warning.

He then cut across the cane fields to the edge of Jenson Cole's house. Unmoving, he sat for an hour watching it. The lights never even came on anywhere in the house. He moved on toward the edge of the cane fields surrounding Fred Cole's home. Here he lay invisibly for another hour as the night came into full bloom.

It was a good night for stalking. The moon was only a sliver hanging in the velvet stars. Winkler saw lights on in this home. Someone was there. The blue flickering glow from a television filled the window of the den. Occasionally, the kitchen light snapped on, shooting a yellow shaft of light out into the night.

Winkler moved in for a closer look. Through the den window he saw two men watching an old Western movie. They were both in their late sixties, and he knew these had to be the eldest Cole brothers, Fred and David. They must have finished their golf and Chinese food and were settling in to watch some old black-and-white film.

When the younger brother, David, shuffled into the kitchen for two more beers, then returned, Winkler knew it was time.

He quickly moved back to the edge of the cane field and took out the notebook and red wax pencil. Guided by the thin shaft of bluish LED light, he wrote the message that Custer had told him to deliver. Ripping it out of the notebook, he slid it into his back pocket, then slipped deeper into the cover of the growing sugarcane. There he left his backpack, taking only his long knife, the LED flashlight, and the red wax pencil.

Winkler started toward the home of Fred Cole.

He checked along the bottom windows along the back. None were unlocked. At the back porch, Winkler tested an ornamental support. It looked like metal ivy leaves growing upward between two metal posts. It held tight, and within seconds he was on the back roof of the home.

He found an unlocked second-story window and slipped in upstairs. The old men must have been hard of hearing—even up on the second floor, Winkler could hear the gunshots and Indian war whoops from the B Western on the TV.

The thought of slipping downstairs and confronting the old men came to him, but Custer had given him specific orders, and he followed them. Using the thin light of the LED flashlight, he found Fred Cole's bedroom and explored it.

Winkler was not without a dry, humorous streak. While there were many places to leave the note, he wanted a special spot that could not be missed. As the flashlight beam passed through the bathroom and bounced off a gleaming glass of water, he knew he had found that spot.

It was only around his brother that Fred Cole felt comfortable not wearing his dentures. As dinner was over, Fred Cole had gone upstairs and plopped them into their nightly resting place, a glass of water.

Winkler took the dentures, emptied the water down the sink, and put the note inside. He turned to leave, then thought of something to add to the warning note. He flattened it out on the sink countertop, added a final sentence, and smiled as he placed the paper back into the glass.

His mission accomplished, Winkler exited the house the way he had entered and was miles away before the note was discovered.

He hiked away from Fred Cole's house toward the highway, wondering how he would get back to Vero Beach. He stumbled across the answer thirty minutes later.

Hidden among one of the cane fields was a small storage building. Winkler's hunter-eyes didn't miss the alarm wires hooked up to the windows. He knew that at least one of the Cole henchmen would come and explore the alarm if it was tripped. He broke the glass with a rock, walked into some chest-high cane close by, and waited.

Fifteen minutes later a Ford F-150 truck pulled up; its headlights cut bright shafts of white light across the front of the building. Grumbling, a man got out of the truck, wondering what had set the alarm off this time. He hated the thing.

There was nothing but fertilizer in the building, and only God knew why the Coles had an alarm on it. Every time it went off, the man was called and had to come down in the middle of the night to find some raccoon or rat had set it off.

So set in his knowledge, and intent on getting back home, the man never suspected that it was a human intruder who had interrupted his watching TV. The man opened the door, turned on the light, and saw nothing but a broken window and the same damn bags of fertilizer that he had seen yesterday.

He pulled out a cell phone, called the alarm company and told them it was a false alarm, then hung up.

Winkler had just intended to take the man down, tape him up, and steal his truck.

The man never knew what hit him as Winkler crept up behind him and kicked his knee joints from behind. The man went down like a dropped sack of potatoes onto the hard concrete of the storeroom floor.

Winkler was on the man's back, pinning him, before the man's breath had fully left his lungs. The man knew he was in trouble when the stalker grabbed his hair, pulled his head back, and put his razor-sharp knife to the man's throat.

"Don't speak. Listen and do," Winkler said. "Slowly, spread your hands out."

The captive quickly complied. Using the electrical tape, Winkler slowly wrapped the man's right wrist many times, then pulled it back behind his back; the Ford's headlights snuck into the room through the door, throwing shadows.

"Owww," the man screamed, "you're breaking my arm."

"I told you not to talk," came the reply, as the left wrist was yanked back and taped. Then both were bound together tightly behind the man's back. Winkler heavily taped the captive's ankles before he stood up.

"I'm taking your truck," he informed the man.

"Do you know who I work for?" the man questioned.

"The Coles."

"Damn right. Know what they'll do to you?" the man spat out the threat.

"They'll never catch me," Winkler replied.

"Yes, we will, you son of a bitch!" came another hollow threat. "You have no idea what we'll do."

Winkler hit the man hard in the ribs.

"I know what you do to preachers," he said. He didn't mind the Cole family finding out that whoever did this also left the note.

The man on the ground was silent under the tracker, surrounded by the headlight beams. A big grin came over his face as if he had just discovered how to slice bread for the first time.

"You're that fella looking for the preacher. That man who disappeared a couple weeks ago." The man beamed. "You were looking for . . ." The man realized he wasn't supposed to talk about that preacher.

"The one looking for what?" Winkler demanded.

"Nothing."

Winkler was down on one knee by the man's side quickly, with his knife back at the man's throat.

"What happened to Preacher Yoder?" he almost whispered.

"Never heard of him," the captive insisted.

Among the numerous ways of the Apache he had trained in, Winkler had studied how to make men talk. Intimidation goes only so far; a little blood travels much deeper through a man's mind. Winkler barely cut the man's cheek.

"If I don't like what I hear, I try a new ear. Yours." He pressed the point of the knife into the jawline just under the captive man's earlobe. "Talk. Everything."

The man broke; the story flowed out like a flood from a shattered dam.

"We went and took him. Six of us one night." The captive blurted it out. "Damn man broke my arm. But there were too many of us. We got him and tied him up."

"And?" The knifepoint went into the skin a millimeter deeper.

"We took him to our warehouse. He was tied up and couldn't move. It was Jenson Cole who ordered it. He showed up after we had him."

"Him. His name was Yoder," Winkler informed the man.

"That's the one. We were supposed to scare him—but he didn't scare. He just sat there staring back at us with anger in his eyes. Usually people pleaded with us, but not that bastard."

As he got involved in the story, the man on the floor almost had pride in his voice.

"We whipped and beat him good. But he still didn't break. We all pissed on him and kicked him like a dog, but nothing."

"What happened to him?" Winkler asked, his voice growing quiet. "Where is he?"

"I don't know."

Winkler used the knife to cut a quarter inch into the man's earlobe.

"I swear it!" the man pleaded. "Ray took me to the hospital for my arm. I saw the rest hauling that man into the back of Jenson's truck."

"And you never asked?"

"You don't ask Jenson Cole nothing. Especially about some man being driven off at midnight in the back of his truck."

"What usually happens?" Winkler questioned.

"I never been involved, but into the lake is what rumor is. They disappear." The man was pleading as his blood ran from his ear. "You never seen any of them again."

Winkler thought for a moment.

"We're going for a walk now," he stated flatly, as he cut the tape on the man's ankles and dragged him to his feet.

He pushed him along out into the cane fields. They soon came to one of the deep, black-water irrigation canals that feed the ever-hungry sugar fields.

"I'm going to leave you here," Winkler told him. "I'll tell the Coles where you are. They will come for you tomorrow."

The man felt relief.

"You pissed on Larry Yoder?" Winkler asked.

"Damn right. And when we catch you, you'll get the same."

"You talk too much."

Winkler didn't hesitate. He yanked the man's head back by his dirty hair and sliced deep through his neck, almost severing the head. Winkler then drove his knife deep into the man's gut so it wouldn't bloat and make him rise in the water. He kicked the dead man down the concrete embankment, watching him slide under the black waters.

The Cole henchman died gasping like a fish out of water.

Winkler didn't even think about killing the man as he drove away. It was as if he had killed a rattlesnake or a rabid dog. It had to be done.

He parked the truck in a hotel parking lot next to the Palm Beach airport, wiped it clean of his prints, and went to a Denny's close by. He called Fred Custer from a pay phone. He then sat and ate breakfast as he waited for someone to come pick him up. It was Hickey who drove down and took him back to Vero Beach.

Right before they left the Denny's parking lot, Winkler took the dead man's cell phone and punched the redial button. A minimum-wage community college student answered the line. Winkler told the kid to give the Coles a message.

"Tell them that the friends of Larry Yoder left a very personal message. It's in the water behind the building where the alarm went off," the usually quiet Winkler said. For him, this was a long speech. "Tell them to read the message carefully. If they don't answer, we'll come back and talk to them in person."

Baffled by the cryptic phone call, the student, who was studying to become an accountant, tried to get more information. Winkler had already slapped the cell phone face closed. When he and Hickey got onto Interstate 95 going north, the quiet tracker opened the window and tossed the cell phone over the top of the Jeep, knowing it would be crushed by the cars and trucks traveling that highway. Then he took the dentures and threw them out, too.

CHAPTER 19

Explosives can be used for many field expedient uses.

—POI 7658 Special Forces Combat Manual ROV 1970

Soon after Fred Cole woke up at 7:00 A.M., all hell broke loose in Belle Glade. With his glasses off, Fred Cole hadn't noticed the note at 3:00 A.M. when he had gotten out of bed to piss, but he sure found it in the early morning light when he went for his dentures.

He read the words in disbelief. That his home had been invaded was bad enough. The fact that someone was actually threatening him and his family was unheard of.

The note read:

This is your last chance to call us and arrange for us to come claim Larry Yoder alive, or his body, if he is dead. We have told you we only want him, alive or dead. We are sincere. Ignore us at your own peril. Call 1-800-555-7945 and leave a message. You have 48 hours. Next time I take more than the teeth.

The last sentence was what Winkler had added while standing in the bathroom.

The 800 number was an answering service in New York City. Once again, by burying the use of that service behind many corporations, Custer had assured that no one, short of a full government investigation, could root out who had hired the answering service to see if the Coles called.

Having been the bullies all their lives, the Coles just could not believe that anyone would challenge their authority on their home ground. The Cole family had run things in Belle Glade for so long, holding each generation of police and town council under their thumb, that the idea of anyone actually standing up to them was as foreign as the president of the United States getting a job at McDonald's after he left office.

Fred Cole called his police department and demanded the chief get to his house right away. Next he called his brother and son and told them he wanted all their foremen at his house.

"I don't care what they're doing. Get them here ten minutes ago!" he yelled into the phone at his eldest child, Jenson. Jenson asked if he was all right—he sounded funny.

"Of course I sound funny. They took my teeth. Now, get going!" Fred Cole slammed the receiver down.

After everyone had arrived and started looking around, of course they destroyed any possibility of finding Winkler's tracks, what few signs there had been. Another seriously experienced tracker could have found them. None of the Cole men or the policemen there had a clue of what to look for in the earth. These officers' idea of police work was a nightstick beating of a cane worker or a trip across the lake at midnight. They were on the payroll for their loyalty, not for their police or forensic skills.

They bumped into each other and tried hiding from the rants

of Fred Cole. Jenson Cole's cell phone rang. It was the head of the alarm security company, passing on the cryptic message from last night. Jenson took three men and some handguns out to the desolate storage building.

It took them thirty minutes of poking around in that black water with a wooden pole to find the body. Jenson Cole ordered the youngest, newest henchman into the water to drag the body out.

"You want me to go in there?" the man asked, smelling the putrid waters.

"Would you rather join him?" came Jenson's cold reply.

The man waded in and slipped as his heel hit the green slime growing on the concrete embankment just under the waterline. He flopped right into the body, and when his eyes saw what was left of the man's neck, he coughed up all the air in his lungs.

As he broke the surface, he spat out the dank water that had filled his mouth. The newest member of the Cole gang tried clawing his way up the rough concrete, back to land. Jenson Cole kicked him back into the water. The man somehow got up enough nerve to grab the dead man's shirt and drag the body out to the edge, where the water lapped against the concrete.

He was even able to drag the body halfway up the embankment, the almost-severed head twisting sideways, the dead man's bulging tongue swollen outside his mouth, before anyone else helped pull the body onto land.

Once back up on dry ground, the new man coughed up more water and looked down, seeing the dead man fully for the first time. He stumbled away, his breakfast quickly rising, and was barely able to make it into a cane field before dropping to his knees and vomiting.

If ever there had been doubt about telling the strangers about Yoder, it ended there. This was the third Cole man killed over the preacher. Staring down at the dead man, Jenson Cole was reminded of the brother and nephew he had just buried, killed by these strangers.

"There won't be another Cole death," Jenson murmured under his breath in a cold, quiet voice, his pupils opening fully until they were black discs like a shark's.

The others standing there knew better than even to speak to Jenson when he was in a black mood like this. They just waited for his orders.

"Get that body into the back of my truck," Jenson ordered, pointing his thumb behind him as he walked away. "Then everyone back to my dad's house."

Back at his father's house, Jenson went inside and found Fred Cole. He took him outside and showed him the corpse.

If Fred Cole was angry before, he was furious now. He screamed and yelled at the top of his lungs, his words often impossible to understand because of his missing teeth. The police chief got the worst of it. For five straight minutes he just stood there, like a private being chewed out by his drill instructor. Fred Cole's rant was punctuated by a forefinger thump onto the chief's chest a few times, and the old man's spittle landed on the chief's face and uniform.

The chief of police thought the old man was going to have a stroke right there, he was so angry. No one had ever seen him go off like this before.

When the chief felt it was safe—Fred Cole had stopped yelling and was bent over, gasping for air—he made the excuse that he had to go get a radio call out on this, and drove away from the house.

Fred Cole straightened up and walked into his house. As he passed Jenson he told him, "Get everyone to the warehouse in one hour."

Every man of Cole family blood, and the foremen and supervisors in their employ, was at the main tin-roofed warehouse by the appointed time. They were all as baffled as before about who was doing this to them. After the death of John Lee Cole and his father, they had prodded the police to find out who the stranger was who had done this.

The police searched but never found a clue.

AT THE SAME TIME THAT the Cole men were meeting in the warehouse, Winkler was briefing all of the men at Custer's house. He told them what had happened, what he had heard and seen, and he showed them the floor plan he had drawn.

The men sat around discussing their next move.

"We wait to see if they call," Custer said.

"They won't," Hickey stated flatly.

"Probably not," Custer countered, "but we'll see. In the meantime I'm going to see what I can find out about this annual get-together."

As the hours ticked by on the forty-eight-hour warning and the New York telephone answering service never got a call, Fred Custer put Judy Wainscott in Miami back on the payroll. Rooting deeply through newspaper archives, she found one reference to the get-together in an article from 1974. It spoke of a local, friendly little party thrown by Belle Glade's most prominent family.

Sometime back in the fifties, the Coles had started the annual event. It was a party on Labor Day, the last official holiday of the summer; a celebration of the coming harvest. What began as a basic family barbecue with a few beers slowly grew into a male-only event with hard liquor, drugs, porn films, and the debauchery that had seeped into the celebration.

The old article she found also had a grainy black-and-white photo. In it, a younger Fred, David, and Jenson Cole smiled back at the lens, all with longneck beer bottles in their hands.

She photocopied the article and image and dropped them off at a Miami delivery service. From there, they were driven directly to Palm Beach, where the quiet man from Orlando appeared again and took delivery of the package. Driving north, he twice made sure no one was following him before he took the Vero Beach exit and handed the package over to Fred Custer.

Now that they knew where all of the Cole men would be at a certain date, they decided to strike on that day. It was a little more than three weeks away. That would be fine, Custer figured. It would give the men time to train some more with the latest equipment he had acquired for them. It would also give the Coles time to think they were safe, that this was all some poker table bluff. Their guard would be lowered when Custer and his men struck.

It took the Miami contracting firm owned by Mitchell Kaplan four days to erect the wooden four-by-fours and two-by-fours with tin sheets hammered on for walls and a roof. Built upon the German man's land, it was the same layout and dimensions as the Cole warehouse. Custer and his men picked up their weapons from the storage facility and added them to their stash of the new night-vision equipment and other items that Fred had bought through the Miami gun dealer.

They were back in the woods and swamps for another week, doing live-fire exercises and practicing an assault on the building. The question was raised of how to get the captive women out of the building before any shooting took place.

Many ideas were kicked around the campfire before Sharkey, this time drinking a stout English beer he had insisted on bringing, came up with a solution.

Hickey took a quick trip to Naples the next day and bought the two items they would need. Back at the camp they tested Sharkey's idea. It worked.

The men planned, plotted, and practiced again and again during the night and during the day. David Hargis became perfect at shooting his .50-caliber rifle from a special perch fifteen feet above the ground. It was another item Custer had bought just for the operation. After a week they were satisfied, so they returned to Vero Beach to make their final preparations.

Another contracting firm, this time out of Tampa, was hired to come pull down the tin structure and drag the debris away to a dump. One week before the assault on the Cole family in Belle Glade, there was no trace that Custer and his men had ever been on the German man's land.

At noon on the day before Labor Day, Fred Custer and his men rolled out of Vero Beach and onto Interstate 95 heading south. They took hotel rooms in the Palm Beach area near the airport and settled in. The next day they would drive into Belle Glade to resolve the issue once and for all.

From a pay phone, Hickey called Jackson, the county officer he had met earlier. He made an appointment to meet him the next day at 2:00 P.M. where they had talked before.

At 2:00 A.M., Winkler, Sharkey, and Hickey drove to another hotel and stole three sets of license plates from vehicles similar to the ones they were driving.

CHAPTER 20

When in position, personnel should keep their equipment on

and remain alert until the perimeter has been checked for

360 degrees at a distance of no less then 40 to 60 meters.

—POI 7658 Special Forces Combat Manual ROV 1970

EACH YEAR THE BELLE GLADE SUGARCANE fields are burned before harvesting the sweet, raw sugar. Each field is burned to destroy any debris before harvesting. Orange fires fill the night as dark smoke and ash float up into the air and spread all over South Florida.

Wild game living in the fields are chased from their homes by these fires. Mostly rabbits, they are harvested by poor laborers using the same machetes with which they will soon cut the cane stalks. The meat is eaten in the cheap apartments or under the tin shacks along the edges of Lake Okeechobee. The better-off locals stun the animals, cut the necks with a sharp knife, then sell the meat at roadside stops to make a few extra dollars for the coming Christmas season. Some of the meat even makes it to metropolitan Miami, where a fresh, fat hare might yield five dollars.

The green stalks of raw sugar had grown almost to their full height for picking. The Coles had laid in a huge feast with kegs of beer and bottles of Jack Daniel's, Absolut, and other hard liquors stacked against the back wall on the wooden table. Bags of cocaine and vials filled with Ecstasy were brought in from Miami's South Beach and added to the goods.

At 6:00 P.M., by which time the partygoers were ready, trucks were sent out with three armed men in each of them. The prettiest women of the migrant workers had already been selected. The trucks rolled up to their apartments or shacks and dragged these women from their peace. Anyone trying to stop this was given a crack against the nose with the butt of a pistol and then shown the barrel. The husbands, fathers, and brothers backed down.

A couple of the men dared to call the police after the event. The police told them that they would investigate in the morning, then hung up and went back to watching the Dolphins game on TV.

The women were placed behind the padlocked door, and the party began in earnest as the sun started to set. All twenty of the Cole family men and the thirty-odd henchmen they employed were there and ready.

After the death of three of the Cole family, and the note to Fred Cole, guards were posted, one at the edge of the cane field on each side of the building. They had pump shotguns, and none of them liked being outside, guarding against nothing as the big party unfolded. They had all seen or heard rumors about the dead man in the water, but they didn't think anything would happen if it hadn't happened already.

Winkler, invisible to their eyes in his camouflage, had been in place since noon. Using a two-way headset, he reported back to Custer that the guards were changed every two hours.

At 2:00 P.M., Hickey drove into Belle Glade. He waited at the edge of the Texaco parking lot until he saw Officer Jackson pull up to the gas pump. Hickey rolled his Jeep to the opposite side, got out, and started pumping gas.

"What would you think if the Cole family went away?" Hickey asked.

"That would be a good day. Never happen, but it would be a good day," the ex-marine replied.

"Jackson, that marine pin on your chest—you were in Beirut, right?"

Jackson looked down to the little red enamel pin on his chest and thought silently about what it stood for, to him.

"Yes, I was," he said, looking up.

"You knew some of the marines who died in that bomb blast," Hickey said. It wasn't a question.

"Of course."

"Well, if you could, what would you do to the men who planned that? The ones who made it happen."

More silence as the gas lines pulsed.

"Kill them," Jackson said, after a moment.

"So would I." Hickey paused. "Jackson, I want you to do something for me."

Jackson studied the bearing of the man before him and waited for the request.

"Something is going to happen. The Cole family goes away soon." Hickey finished filling his tank and stopped the pump. He stared straight at Jackson's eyes. "This will happen, Jackson, and we don't want anything going wrong. We certainly don't want any civilians or county officers getting in the way. I'm asking you to keep your county law brothers away, Jackson. We are well armed, and this will happen. You'll know when it goes down. All we are asking for is a few hours, after you hear about it. We'll do this thing, and then we go away forever."

Hickey pulled the nozzle out and replaced it on the pump.

"Who are you?" Jackson asked.

"Enemies of the Coles," Hickey replied. "Can I count on you, Jackson?"

Jackson stared back, silent.

"Think of Beirut." Hickey slapped his palm atop the pump. "This time, the good guys do it right."

"Just the Coles?" Jackson asked.

"Them and their henchmen only," Hickey stated.

Another quiet moment.

"OK," Jackson agreed, remembering his grandparents and parents and all the others he had heard about who had suffered under the brutal family.

Hickey could see the truth in the man's eyes. He pulled his palm away from the pump and held it out.

"Thanks, Jackson." They shook hands.

Hickey got into his Jeep and smiled at the man who had just decided to ignore his badge and see if the world would be better for that action. He reached over and held another disposable cell phone out toward the man. Jackson took it.

"You keep that on for the next week from 6:00 P.M. to 11:00 P.M. I'll call you when it's over. See you around, maybe, Jackson." Hickey smiled.

"Could be," Jackson said.

He watched the stranger in the Jeep drive away.

Jackson drove out and warned his fellow officers that Belle Glade was off-limits for a week. He drove around and found them one by one, and they talked from one cruiser to another. He told them just to shy away from the Cole family's places for a few nights.

The soft words he spoke to fellow officers were powerful. The stripes on Jackson's sleeves spoke of his experience on the force; but, more important, the regard the other field officers had for the man did the job. They would wait to hear from Jackson.

While he did that, Hickey called the Reverend Mark Janus at his home. His home telephone number was listed as an "emergency number" on the business card Hickey had taken. He figured this qualified. He asked the man to meet him at his church.

When Janus pulled up, Hickey told him to spread the word through the workers and poor. Stay home at night, starting tonight. No matter what they heard or saw, they should stay home. Don't alert any of the Cole people, just the real workers, their families, and the poor—his flock. This was a matter of life and death.

"You know who made Pastor Yoder disappear?" Hickey asked the man.

"I have my suspicions."

"Well, Reverend, we have a lot more than suspicions, and we're going to do something serious about it," Hickey warned the man. "We don't want any innocents in the way."

Hickey handed the man a piece of paper with a cryptic "Ex. 22:24" written on it. Pastor Mark Janus knew the quote.

Hickey had convinced him. Word was spread.

Reverend Mark Janus got home just after dinnertime. He had driven around and spoken to the men and women among the poor, and to cane workers who, he knew, would pass quiet warnings. Telephones rang, children were sent running across open fields with messages, and word was passed.

His chore done, he pulled his favorite Bible down and opened it to Exodus and found chapter 22, verse 24. He knew the words by heart, but seeing them on the old vellum paper under his fingers assured him he had done the right thing. He read them silently to himself, and a shiver ran down his spine. He read the words aloud.

"And my wrath shall wax hot, and I will kill you with the sword; and your wives shall be widows, and your children fatherless."

Mark Janus went and prayed for the souls of Belle Glade,

even the Coles. He knew something serious was going to happen within the next week.

AT 4:00 P.M., FOUR MASKED, well-armed men walked into the Belle Glade Police Department headquarters. They were wearing overcoats, and when the desk officer saw AK-47s, M-16s, and a Colt .45 swing out from under the coats and aim at him, he froze.

The four men quickly rounded up and disarmed the three officers on duty. The officers were in their own handcuffs in less than two minutes. All three were taken to the jail cells and placed there.

"Who runs the radio?" Hickey asked.

"Billy, here." One of the men nodded over to his left.

"Come on, Billy," Hickey commanded, and the man was taken to the radio.

"Call whoever is on patrol back here now, Billy," Hickey ordered him, before letting one of Billy's cuffed wrists free. "Get them here. Tell them the chief wants to see them now."

Billy was shaking as he took the microphone and pressed the button to speak.

"Billy," Hickey said calmly.

Billy looked up with fear in his eyes.

"Billy, nothing is going to happen to you as long as you play it smart," Hickey soothed the young man. "But we are prepared, Billy. We are far better armed then any of your force. So don't do anything stupid, Billy. Just get them here. You don't want their blood on your hands, do you?"

"No, sir," Billy said.

Billy did as he was told.

When the two officers on patrol were added to the jail cells, Hickey had Billy call the three off-duty officers. Billy told them it was an emergency, and he was not lying. These men arrived, and, one by one, they were locked behind their own bars.

Finally, Hickey had Billy call the chief of police at home.

"What the hell's up that's so damned important?" he asked. "I just got home and got my shoes off."

"It's an emergency, sir," Billy got out before Hickey disconnected the call.

It took the chief ten minutes to get there, and within five minutes every officer of the Belle Glade police force was handcuffed tight and locked behind bars.

The four masked men ignored their questions as they slammed and locked the heavy steel door separating the cells from the outer offices. They had every handcuff key, car key, cell door key, and outer door key in their possession. They locked the outside doors and drove away.

By 6:00 P.M., they had changed into their camo uniforms with the thick Kevlar body armor underneath and were waiting for Fred Custer's call.

As dusk took over, and Custer was talking to Winkler, the trucks with the captured women had all returned to the warehouse. The women were locked in the room, and the guards had just been changed.

It was time.

CHAPTER 21

Once you have committed yourself and sprung
your ambush, you must be aggressive.

—POI 7658 Special Forces Combat Manual ROV 1970

Go! GO!" WERE THE ONLY WORDS Custer's men heard crackling over their headsets.

Hickey, Winkler, and Sharkey each moved through the cane around them. Each man approached a guard on the sides and back of the structure. The music from inside the building grew as they all inched closer to their first targets.

The guards, having already been inside, were slightly drunk and hardly alert. One of them had even sat down, putting his shotgun on the ground, and had closed his eyes. He would have fallen asleep had Hickey's hands not grabbed him and yanked him behind the cover of the sugarcane stalks.

The chloroform had him fully asleep within a minute. First, Hickey used plastic handcuffs on the man's wrists, and then he duct-taped over those. The sticky, thick tape was then triple-wrapped tightly around the man's ankles. He was out of action for the night.

Hickey spoke into his microphone. "First gator roped," he said.

Winkler and Sharkey had similar success with their guards. They replied with the same words on the team's private radio net, adding "second" and "third" to their respective "gators."

"Broken arrow," Custer replied.

Those words began phase two.

Winkler moved down the edge of the field just inside the covering stalks and grabbed a heavy Fred Bear bow he had laid on the ground. With the wide double doors exposing forty feet of open doorway, he had an easy view into the building. He notched a long arrow with a piece of paper wrapped and rubber-banded around its shaft and pulled the bowstring back taut. He held the eighty-pound pull like a rock.

Hickey took a full five-gallon gasoline can and spread the gas around the field in which he stood. The gas covered the area where an Estes rocket fuse waited. He lit the fuse and ran, moving around the perimeter to join Sharkey on the side of the warehouse where the room with the women was located.

"Baker ready," he whispered into his plastic headset, once he was in place.

Dan Hadad sprang out of the edge of the cane and grabbed the guard in front of the building and pulled him deep into the cane stalks. Before the man could yell out, Hadad had a chloroform-steeped rag over his mouth. He held it tight until he knew the guard was out. Hadad then bound him up tight. It was over in less than two minutes.

"Fourth gator roped," Hadad said, pulling up his M-16 with the grenade launcher mounted underneath the weapon's barrel.

He crouched on one knee and aimed carefully into the center of the large warehouse and waited.

One of the men standing in the open doors, watching the sun fading away, thought he saw movement at the edge of the field where the guard had just disappeared. Without his glasses he couldn't be sure. Then he saw a fire in the cane field to his right.

"No one is supposed to be burning tonight," he said aloud to himself. He was just about to turn and mention what he had seen when it all let loose.

"Western Union," Custer stated. "Western Union."

Winkler let the arrow fly. The tin walls were no target, so he picked something the men inside would notice: the porn movie playing on an eighty-four-inch projection TV.

It was interrupted as the sturdy arrow shaft buried itself deep inside the reflective material of the television screen.

"What the hell?" David Cole got out of his chair and stared at the arrow, wondering where it had come from.

Fred Cole saw the paper and reached up and yanked the shaft. The steel, four-headed hunting arrowhead had done its job: It was buried too deeply to come out. Fred Cole just broke the shaft and brought it to his belly. He took the note off and read it under the undulating light of the film.

Last chance. Give us Yoder, was all the note had penned on it.

As Fred Cole read the words, their implications sank into his vodka-filled head. Winkler was lighting another Estes fuse as he quickly snaked away to join Hadad in front of the building. Once he had his Stoner rifle in his hands, he spoke into the headset again.

"Package delivered."

Fred Custer was giving the Cole men one more chance. He was still willing to walk away if they turned over Larry Yoder.

Winkler and Hadad both saw the response they would get. Fred Cole was yelling, getting his men organized. He had to shut off the movie and the music boom box to get their attention.

"They're here!" he warned. "The bastards are outside!"

The Cole men slowly responded from their various states of drunkenness or drug stupor.

"Get the guns!" Fred Cole ordered, running over to the room where the shotguns, rifles, and pistols were stored. He unlocked it, and one by one all the weapons were handed out. By now, the fires were building as the rows of dry cane caught. The smoke began to roll up into the air.

"Negative Geneva. That's negative Geneva," Hadad reported, referring to the famed city where peace treaties are signed.

"Cry havoc," came Custer's command to go to the next level of their plan. "Cry havoc."

Dan Hadad and Winkler fired their grenade launchers, and the two stun grenades exploded in the middle of the room. They reloaded and let loose two rounds of tear gas.

The Cole men grabbed their ears, fell to the ground, and were generally incapacitated by the stun grenade rounds. The rounds were not designed to kill, but merely to make anyone in the place wish he had been somewhere else. Now two things happened.

First, Dave Hargis rolled down the road between the cane fields, driving a Chevy pickup that Geraldine had found on Craigslist. The truck had a steel frame tower welded onto the bed. On top of that, fifteen feet from the ground, was a bench seat easily big enough for two men to sit atop.

This was a truck built for deer hunting. A four-wheel-drive deer blind was what Fred Custer had bought from a man who was moving to Michigan. They had picked it up two weeks ago, and Fred had handed the man cash.

The deer blind became Fred Custer's command post and Dave Hargis's shooting stand. With Custer firmly belted atop the bench seat, Hargis drove the truck behind the Coles' warehouse a good football field away and parked facing it. Hargis then climbed up to his sniper's perch where his Barrett .50 rifle waited. He would watch the back door and stop anyone who tried getting out that way.

He knew where the rest of the team was and where he could and could not send his deadly .50-caliber rounds.

The other thing that happened was that Hickey and Sharkey came crashing out from the edge of the rows of cane, each man wielding a chainsaw. As soon as they were at the warehouse wall, they yanked the cords and brought the saws to life.

Hearing the sounds of the whirring chain saws over their headsets, Hadad and Winkler let go with two more stun grenades into the warehouse. Then they faded back into the cane fields, shifted left and right away from each other, and slid behind some protective berms they had built up during the day. They dropped into the three-foot-deep ditches they had dug behind the berms. No bullet fired from the warehouse would find them. If the Cole men started firing in the direction from which the grenade shots had come, they would hit nothing but the spot where the two soldiers had been. Winkler dropped the M-16 and grabbed his favored Stoner rifle.

Hickey and Sharkey carved right through the thin metal side of the warehouse and had soon created a new door. They threw the chain saws down and peeled back the metal.

They stared into a small room where terrified women were braced against the door and wondering what was going on.

"English?" Hickey yelled above the noise. "Anyone speak English?"

"Yes." A woman looked back at him. Unlike the rest of the women, she didn't have the look of fear of a deer caught in headlights. Hickey pointed behind himself to the open fields.

"Tell them to get moving. That way," he told her. "Run. Now. Get the hell away from here."

The woman hesitated only a second. His cold blue eyes told her more than his words did. There was menace in the man's gaze. She translated to the other women as Sharkey stepped into the room and started pushing the women out the hole in the wall.

"Go. Now," Hickey commanded. "Run as fast and as far as you can."

With the woman talking to them in Creole and Sharkey pushing them out, the women and girls were soon outside and moving away from the danger. As the last woman made it out, the one who spoke English, Hickey grabbed her by the arm, turning her to face him.

"Stay together. Keep moving. Don't stop." He stared into her eyes.

She had seen many hard men in her life. This man had that look in his eyes.

"Yes," she replied.

Hickey released her arm. "Go now!"

As the women made it away, Hickey and Sharkey also got out. Their AK-47s at the ready, they moved along the perimeter in opposite directions. Sharkey positioned himself just inside the cane field's edge, to the side of the building facing the front right corner. Anyone coming out of the doors or even out of the new escape door they had chain-sawed was his assignment.

Hickey ran around the back perimeter, seeing Custer and Hargis in place in the rear, and positioned himself farther down the line opposite Sharkey. Neither wanted to be in the other's line of fire.

"Freedom bird airborne," Hickey barked into his headset. The women were free and running.

Everyone on the team radio net knew the women were safe now. There was nothing but enemies in the kill zone.

None of the men inside the warehouse had any idea of the new hole in the side of the structure. The sound of the chain saws was more than drowned out in the aftermath of the exploding grenades.

The Cole men were boxed in all around by trained soldiers and some massive firepower waiting to be unleashed if needed.

David Hargis took careful aim and let half the air out of his lungs. He had his target, and he waited for the shot. The .50 boomed into the fading light of dusk. The big ceramic insulator on the back of the building shattered, and the heavy power line was severed. The live wire fell to the ground, and all the electricity inside the building went out.

As the Cole men started to panic, every one of Custer's men except Hargis slipped on his night-vision goggles and waited as the eerie green light filled their vision. Hargis was staring through a night-vision scope mounted atop the heavy rifle frame.

With this advantage, Custer and his men now had the total battlefield: They owned the night. They could see all the Cole men in their vision as ghostly green blurs, and the Cole men could see nothing of them.

Fred Cole hadn't taken over and run the family empire ever since Poppa Cole had died without knowing how to get those working for him moving.

"Shoot back!" he yelled, pulling a 12-gauge shotgun to his shoulder and letting a round off in the direction where Hadad and Winkler had been moments before. The buckshot spread out, ripping into the sugarcane stalks.

A couple of the other men joined in, and then every man there with a weapon in his hands was in a line, firing out into the empty field. Their line of fire lit up the dark and deafened all the men inside the building.

While Hadad and Winkler hugged the earth, an occasional stray round flying above them, the dry cane stalks took the brunt of the Cole gang's assault. The cane cracked and snapped under the lead bullets and steel shot. The untrained men inside the warehouse had made a huge mistake. They had all emptied their weapons into the field. More than one man continued pulling a trigger with an empty chamber. As soon as the gunfire from inside had stopped, Custer's team returned fire.

Unlike the shots from the frightened men inside the warehouse, those from the weapons that let loose from the field outside were specific and deadly. Trained soldiers opened up, each with thousands of hours' experience behind his gun. It was a turkey shoot: All the men they were shooting at were inside a metal box, with nowhere to run.

Sharkey and Hickey opened up from the sides and in front of the building; their deadly 7.62×33 mm bullets flew from the assault rifles at six hundred rounds per minute. Hearing the distinctive sound of the AK-47 to their sides, Winkler and Hadad rose up and leveled their Stoner and M-16 rifles and pulled triggers. In less then two seconds, both fired, Hadad sending a fragmentation grenade mounted on the bottom of his weapon and Winkler sending a stream of 5.56 mm rounds dancing across the room. Hadad sent another frag into the warehouse space.

Before the rounds had landed and the grenade had exploded, both men had dropped back down into their trenches.

The effects of any fragmentation grenade would be deadly enough to a group of men close together in the open. The Cole men were boxed in, and the effects of the two grenades could only be called devastating.

Hot metal shards flew through the air, ripping a path of death through the building. Some of the razor-sharp fragments punched holes through the thin tin walls, but mostly, human flesh absorbed the flying metal.

Sharkey and Hickey kept dropping empty thirty-round clips, slamming fresh ones into the weapons, and unloading those into the warehouse. From his perch above, Dave Hargis was sending the massive .50-caliber rounds downward and through the back wall. He just walked his nine rounds across the back of the building, aiming about six feet above the ground, reloaded a fresh clip, and reversed the path of the next nine shots. More than one Cole man felt the death blow of those large bullets.

Between those rounds and the grenades, most of the men inside were either dead or severely wounded. After the AK-47 fire stopped, the groans of the wounded and dying seeped out of the enclosed space. Amplified from bouncing around inside the tin walls, their cries sounded ghostlike in the night.

There were still survivors, and Fred Cole was among them. Wounded by grenade shrapnel—the man standing beside him had taken most of the flying metal—Fred Cole looked around. One of his foremen was dazed, but somehow untouched.

"Get more ammo passed around!" Fred Cole yelled at him.

Too confused to do anything but obey his boss, the man ran into the storage room and started grabbing boxes of ammo. He had filled his arms with too many boxes. Running back into the main room, he dropped some, the thin cardboard breaking like eggshells on a kitchen floor. Brass rounds spilled useless across the concrete.

Fred Cole grabbed a box of 12-gauge shells from the room, reloaded his shotgun, and filled his pockets with more ammo. He looked around and saw another supervisor whose name he didn't even know.

"You!" Fred Cole barked. "Get them doors closed!"

"No way I'm stepping out there . . ."

Boom! Fred Cole's shotgun spoke, sending the man down hard onto the concrete floor. Cole saw another man who could walk.

"Get them doors closed!" he yelled, pointing the shotgun.

The man reluctantly went over and started to slide the massive door closed on its large rubber wheels. He made it six inches before the ex–British soldier's deadly fire cut him down, four bullets ripping deep into his chest. The man was dead before he hit the ground.

Fred Cole started firing blindly back into the night. A couple of other men joined him. Then Cole saw Jenson, in a sitting position, his back leaning against the rear tin wall. He had taken an AK round through the gut.

"Jenson?" Fred Cole questioned, as he moved toward his boy. His son had his hand pressed against his gut.

"It hurts, Dad," Jenson said, looking up at his father.

"Have your cell phone?" was Fred Cole's response.

Dazed by the wound, Jenson tried to comprehend the logic of the request. "Yeah," he said, in a dopey voice.

"Call the police, boy. Get them here."

Jenson Cole fumbled his cell phone out of his pocket and got it open, his bloody fingers staining the plastic buttons. He tried getting a signal, but yet another one of the items Fred Custer had bought was in effect: An industrial cell signal jammer was hooked up to a series of large car batteries in the back of the deer-hunting truck. It more than covered the combat zone, preventing any cell phones from working. The Coles were on their own this time.

From his command perch, Custer saw something in the field they might use. He got on the headset and gave Winkler an order. At once Winkler was out of his trench and running through the cane fields like a lion chasing down a gazelle.

Hadad also moved. He left the safety of his foxhole and headed over to Hickey. They used the headsets to talk until they were together and shifted away from where Hickey had been firing. They didn't want to stay long where they had been shooting. The fully automatic rifles let off too much flash as the rounds were fired. Trained men would spot these and zero in with counterfire. Even though none of the Cole men were professionally trained, Custer's men didn't take any chances they didn't have to.

As Jenson was trying to figure out why his cell phone wouldn't work, Fred Cole reloaded. He turned to face the open doors again and saw his brother. David Cole had taken a round through the center of his throat; it had punched a pinky-sized hole right through his windpipe.

Slumped against the base of the big-screen TV, gasping for breath, David Cole had wrapped his hand around his throat. Blood flowed out of the hole with every heartbeat. Fred bent down to his dying brother.

"Get them fuckers, Fred" were the last words David Cole croaked out.

Enraged, Fred Cole turned and fired his shotgun uselessly into the night and reloaded.

The men who could still move panicked and tried to escape.

Some just ran out into the night, while a couple tried for their trucks or cars parked outside. They weren't organized. This was a shattered enemy.

Lit up in the night through the night-vision goggles, each man was cut down once he was in the open. Hargis and Hickey used controlled three-round bursts now. They fired and moved. Fired and moved. Every minute or so, a man would try to escape out the open front doors, only to be cut down.

One man actually made it inside his pickup truck. He was crying as he fumbled for his keys, dropping them out of his shaking hand. As the man felt in the dark on the floorboard for them, Sharkey opened up his AK-47, using alternating incendiary and armor-piercing rounds. Like a master carpenter carving wood, he cut his bullets through the gas tanks and tires of the vehicles outside. A tracer round went through a gas tank, and a bright pyre shot up into the sky.

The crying man died as his truck blossomed into a fireball in the night.

One man unlocked the back door and ran out, only to be cut down by Hargis's deadly fire. A minute later a second man saw the open rear door and tried for freedom. The .50-caliber round destroyed his chest and sent him flying back into the room. No one else tried escaping that way.

What Custer had seen in the field, and what he had sent Winkler after, was a large harrow. Built on a John Deere tractor, two rows of spinning discs spread twenty feet out on each side like wings on a bird. After the annual harvesting this tractor would be worked back and forth across the ash-covered fields, turning the earth.

Always one to improvise when possible, Custer had seen the hulk lurking a hundred yards away from the warehouse. Custer saw Winkler move around the edge of the spreading field fires and hop onto the machine.

Winkler thought he would have to hot-wire the tractor, but he found the keys in the ignition. The Coles assumed that no one would ever steal one of their pieces of machinery. People around Belle Glade knew better than to do that.

Winkler was not from around Belle Glade.

The engine roared to life, and Winkler jammed levers and worked pedals until the tractor was moving forward. He pushed the accelerator to the floor, letting the machine build up speed. As it crashed through the rows of cane, he aimed it toward the side of the warehouse.

Winkler jumped from the tractor a few feet before it slammed into the building wall, its momentum and weight ripping the walls open like a tin can. The right-side discs caught against a steel support beam, and the entire tractor turned but kept going. A corner of the building was ripped apart, and the metal fell down atop the machine, stopping it.

Fred Cole literally saw his world falling apart around him. He roared as he charged out the front door, his shotgun blazing, running toward an empty field.

It was Hickey's bullets that cut the old man down and ended his rule.

Silence took over the night. Custer's men cleared each other on the radio net and confirmed that none of them had even taken a hit. They sat waiting to see if anyone else would try an attack.

When no other shots came from within the warehouse, Hickey and Hadad ran up to the front corner and waited, their weapons pointed and ready. Sharkey took a prone position at an angle in front of the building, with a clear field of fire into it.

Winkler had his AK-47 ready as he approached from behind the building, where the tractor had opened a hole. The sounds of the wounded could be heard by all. The smell of cordite and death filled the air.

When they were all in place, Hickey spoke.

"Anyone alive in there, throw out your weapons and then come out with your hands on top of your heads."

One by one, the men who could still move came to the door and tossed their guns out. Only eight of the Cole men walked or crawled out of the bloodbath.

"When you get ten feet outside the building," Hickey yelled again, "lie facedown, hands behind your backs."

They all did it.

Now was the most dangerous part of the operation. They would have to go into the building, exposing themselves to gunfire.

"Guinness up," Hickey whispered into his headset.

Sharkey rose and came over to cover the men lying on the ground, so that no one in the building could get a shot at Hickey.

"Any of you blokes so much as twitch and I kill you," he warned the prisoners in his thick British accent.

"We're coming in. Don't try anything," Hickey announced to the wounded men inside.

Winkler used the new hole the tractor had made in the building to move into the back of the warehouse. He snuck into the back corner of the space and got the muzzle of his weapon pointed into the room. If he saw any man's arms come up with a gun, he would shoot.

"Got you covered, Hickey," he whispered into his headset.

Slowly, with their muzzles facing forward, Hickey and Hadad moved away from the corner protection to barely behind the doors.

"We're coming in. Anyone who tries anything dies," Hickey warned.

Winkler saw the green glow of one man's arms and the warm glow from a rifle barrel coming up and leveling toward the door. Winkler sent three rounds into the man. Hickey knew the sound of an M-16 and figured out what had happened.

"Anyone else a hero?" Hickey roared after a moment.

"For God's sake, no," one wounded man screamed out. "No more."

"How's it look, Winkler?" Hickey asked.

"As good as we'll get," came the reply.

"We're going in. Where are you at in there?"

"One o'clock, far corner," Winkler whispered back into the headpiece.

Hickey went first, quickly running around the edge of the door and slamming his back against the inside of it. Through the night-vision goggles, the bodies of the dead and wounded were like fireflies that were not moving. The glow from a few of the bodies was fading away—they had died first, and their body temperature was dropping. Hickey saw no threatening moves.

"Clear," he said.

Hadad ran in and planted himself in the inside far corner before he slowly moved his weapon's muzzle around the room, looking for any movement. Hickey lifted up the night-vision goggles and let his natural night vision slowly adapt. Winkler came in closer, covering the shattered remains of the Cole family from behind.

He and Hadad also removed their goggles and waited.

As this was going on, Hargis was helping get Custer down from the seat on the deer truck. Once his leader was secure inside the truck cab, Hargis drove it around in front of the building, letting the high beams and spotlights fill the space with light.

The carnage was complete. Blood and exploded flesh filled their eyes and covered the floor and walls. One man who had taken two rounds through his stomach was crawling across the concrete. The truck's headlights lit up the trail of blood and viscera he left behind him.

There was no fight left in any of these men.

Custer's team went to work. They went from man to man. If one stood a chance of living, they patched him up. Trained medics all, Custer's men knew who might make it and who wouldn't. The weapons were all thrown into a corner.

It was Winkler who found Jenson Cole and treated his gut wound.

"He'll live," he announced.

While they were treating the wounded, Sharkey took off, as Hadad covered the men outside. He ran to where they had parked earlier and brought Hickey's Jeep to the front of the warehouse. Then he went back and brought around the Land Rover he had driven down from Vero Beach.

With Jenson alive, they knew they would finally resolve the question of Larry Yoder.

"Handcuff him and put him in my Jeep," Hickey ordered.

The rest of the Cole men were also handcuffed, hogtied, and left facedown in the dirt in front of the warehouse. There were thirteen survivors. Only Jenson Cole remained from the rotten Cole family tree.

Having finished, Custer and his men rolled away from the kill zone.

A growing breeze blew across the fields, spreading the fires. The cane burned until noon the next day. By then, everything that could burn had finished burning.

CHAPTER 22

Stay alert at all times. You are never 100%
safe until you are back home.

—POI 7658 Special Forces Combat Manual ROV 1970

CUSTER TRANSFERRED TO THE PASSENGER SEAT in the Jeep, and Hickey drove. Jenson Cole sat groaning in the back, his gut wound making his insides pulse with pain. Winkler sat next to the handcuffed man, making sure the dressings over the bullet wound didn't leak too much.

Most men who have been shot agree that the gut wound is the most painful. Like any bullet wound causing internal damage, it is often fatal, but it can take days for the wounded man to die. Many wounded that way and untreated beg to be put out of their misery.

Without treatment, Jenson Cole would die after days of constant pain, but Winkler's medical training and bandages had assured that he wouldn't die that night: Jenson Cole would tell them where Larry Yoder was.

Dave Hargis drove away in the deer-hunting truck. It was not an unusual sight on the rural Florida roads, as deer season was quickly approaching. Sharkey followed in the used Land Rover. They drove to the other side of the lake, and Hargis crashed through the deep brush, burying the odd truck deep in the woods on the German's land. Then he hopped into the Land Rover, and the two men headed back to Vero Beach. The truck would sit for seven years before anyone ever saw it again.

As Hickey drove away from the charnel house they had left behind, Fred Custer punched in the cell number of the phone Jackson was carrying and handed the phone over to Hickey.

When the former marine answered, Hickey explained quickly that it had happened. County Officer Jackson hadn't expected word for a day or two. The speed of action of the stranger at the gas pump surprised him.

When he heard the extent of that action, he was stunned.

Hickey told him about the women on the run somewhere, the Belle Glade policemen all locked in their own jail, and the location of the Cole warehouse where the Cole men were waiting to be buried or treated.

"I know that place. How many are there?" Jackson asked after a long moment.

"We counted fifty-four," Hickey stated.

"Dead?"

"At least thirty," Hickey calmly explained.

More silence. Jackson thumped down into his living room chair.

"You got the Coles" was all Jackson could think aloud.

"If there are any left alive, they are all yours," Hickey stated. "Maybe I'll see you around, Jackson."

"Maybe so," came the reply.

Hickey killed the connection. Jackson just sat staring at the cell phone. It took him ten minutes before he even moved. Wearing a shell-shocked look on his face, he slowly walked into the kitchen, and past his wife, mumbling, "They got the Coles."

His wife had no idea what her loving husband was talking about. Officer Jackson dressed in his county uniform and kissed her good-bye before heading out to his car.

He heard the first reports of fires over his police radio as he started the engine. There were also reports of "gunfire like the Fourth of July," and questions were being shot back and forth. The fire department was already rolling to the spreading fires. Once they saw the growing blazes, they started calling in support from the counties around Belle Glade. It was going to be a long night of work.

As Jackson slowly drove toward the warehouse, he started calling the other county officers on patrol. He was the first to arrive, and his headlights covered the men lying, handcuffed and hogtied, across the front of the building.

His blue and red lights danced across the interior of the building. Jackson hefted his long Maglite in his left hand and his Glock 9 mm pistol in his right and slowly entered the charnel house.

Jackson had seen combat. He had seen death in the military and as an officer of the law. He had even seen mass death, pulling shattered bodies and broken limbs of his fellow marines out from under the tons of rubble after the bomb blast in Beirut.

Since then, Officer Jackson had never seen anything like the total carnage his flashlight beam danced across that night. He prayed he would never see anything like it again.

He went back to his car and called in every ambulance he could raise. By midnight, they had also contacted every funeral home within fifty miles to haul away the dead and stack them, like cords of wood, in the county morgue.

Everyone involved agreed, it was the bloodiest event ever in the history of Belle Glade and possibly in the history of Florida. They also agreed that those who suffered here got what they deserved.

SAFELY AWAY NOW, CUSTER TURNED to face Jenson Cole.

"What happened to Larry Yoder?"

"Fuck you" was the response.

Winkler sent a hard fist into the gut of the man, amplifying the already deep pain of his gunshot wound.

Jenson Cole was asked three times, always refusing to tell them anything. Winkler grew tired of the banter. He grabbed Jenson's neck in one tight hand and pinned the man's head against the headrest. With his other hand, he pressed his knife point against the man's breast above the heart. Winkler leaned over and whispered in Jenson Cole's ear.

He whispered for two straight minutes, slapping Jenson's face to stop him twice when Jenson tried to speak.

Hickey's eyebrows rose and he stared over at Custer. Neither of the men had ever heard the quiet man speak that long at once. Fred shrugged his shoulders.

Neither Fred nor Hickey could hear the words, but whatever Winkler said created the desired effect. Jenson Cole's bulging eyes turned in fear, looking at the man who held him tight. He broke quickly.

"He's dead," Jenson Cole croaked out, from beneath Winkler's firm grip around his throat. "We killed him."

"Where's the body?" Custer asked.

"In the lake where I wish I had put you," Cole spat out, looking at Hickey.

"We'll use your boat," Hickey responded. "Tell me where to go."

Looking back over toward Winkler first, Jenson Cole gave Hickey directions to the family docks on the lake.

A BIG YAMAHA OUTBOARD ENGINE pushed the jet-black Ranger 520VX bass boat through the waters of Lake Okeechobee. It was well past 10:00 P.M. now, and the men had the lake all to themselves. They could see the billowing smoke from the orange-yellow fires that spread across the fields, their eerie glow filling the horizon. A handheld spotlight on the boat sent a shaft of light onto the lake.

Custer had stayed behind in the Jeep while Winkler prodded Jenson Cole along, down the wooden pier and into the speedy fishing boat. Winkler carried a small duffle bag in his hand.

Hickey dropped behind the wheel and brought the engine alive while Winkler undid the ropes holding the boat tight to the pier. They were soon on the lake. Winkler added thick wraps of duct tape around Jenson Cole's ankles.

"Which way?" was all Hickey wanted to know.

"Northwest," Cole grumbled back. He hardly wanted to go along, but he had no choice. Whatever Winkler had said to him was still buzzing around in his brain.

"That's kind of a general direction on a thirty-mile by thirty-mile lake," Hickey commented.

"Well, it's not like we have a special place," Cole stated, fighting back any way he could. "We just dump them out here."

Winkler locked his eyes onto the wounded man.

"He's telling the truth," he said.

"Well, we have all night to find him," Hickey stated.

If the Cole family felt a man "needed a bath," as they called it, the man was taken out on the boat on a night like this, mouth taped shut, wrists and ankles tightly bound. Then a chain was wrapped around the center support of a large cinder block; next, the chain was tightly wrapped around the man's ankles and padlocked in place.

He was then dropped over the side, if everyone on board was

through hitting or kicking him. Then the Coles would sit above the spot, smoking cigars and drinking beer, until the cigars were finished. That usually took fifteen minutes. None of the weighed-down men had ever come back up.

There were two cinder blocks and chains in the front storage areas of the boat.

Whenever Jenson Cole told them to, Hickey cut the big engine and Winkler dropped the much smaller trolling motor into the water. It was mounted in front of the boat and pulled them along at slow speeds.

Jenson had to explain to Hickey how to use the depth finder, but once Hickey understood it, he had no problems. They barely moved across the spots where Cole thought the family might have dumped a body, until Hickey would get an unusual spike in the depth finder. That would mean something was sticking up off of the bottom.

Hickey would cut the engine then. Winkler would open the duffle bag he had brought along. He would kick off his boots, strip off his shirt and heavy Kevlar vest, then stand on the foredeck in just his camo pants. He would slip on a scuba mask. He had an underwater flashlight in one hand and a foot-long metal tube in his other.

The tube was a can of Spare Air, designed for emergency use by scuba divers. Screwed on top of the canister of compressed air was a breathing regulator. If a diver's tanks ran dry, he could grab his bottle of Spare Air and get to the surface. Depending on the depth, the air easily lasted fifteen minutes. Custer had bought four cans at a Tampa dive shop.

Falling backward off the bass boat, Winkler would plunge into the cold lake water and swim down. The light would look like a wide laser cutting through the dark, murky waters. The water was forty to sixty feet deep where he explored, but with the compressed air he would find the anomaly that had pinged their depth finder. This time it was an old sunken boat.

Winkler broke the surface, reported, and climbed back on the deck. The search went on.

While Winkler was underwater the second time, Cole spoke up.

"Why did you do this?" he asked Hickey.

"You really don't know, do you?" Hickey replied.

"No," came the reply.

Hickey thought for a moment. He could try to explain to the man about a friendship that went back over thirty years, about bonds that would make a man die for another man. Bonds that ran deeper than life and death because, as brothers in arms, they had faced death daily. Hickey and all the men around him that night understood those bonds, the debts owed and paid among themselves so many times.

Hickey saw that trying to explain all of that to a man like Jenson Cole was like trying to talk to a rat in your kitchen, telling it why it shouldn't steal the cheese.

"Ask God when you see Him" was Hickey's only response.

They found a large mound of silt, a stack of fifty-five-gallon drums, a 1953 Chevy pickup—no one could explain how that made it a quarter mile offshore—and a rusting refrigerator before Winkler found the first Cole victim. It wasn't Yoder.

The next stop yielded three of the chained corpses, swaying back and forth in the current, their bodies in different states of decay. Larry Yoder floated in the middle of the other two.

Winkler broke the surface and looked up at Hickey.

"Found him."

Hickey walked up to the duffle bag and pulled out one of the hundred-yard rappelling ropes they had brought along. He threw the bulk of the rope overboard to Winkler, wrapped his end of the rope around the base of the fishing chair in the bow, and tied it off tight.

Winkler swam back down to the bottom and snaked the rope through one of the cinder-block holes and tied the rope end tight upon itself in a knot.

He followed the rope back up. When he got onto the deck, he

and Hickey pulled the heavy body back to the surface. They were reverent with the body of their friend. They didn't know what state of decomposition it was in, and they didn't want body parts breaking off.

As if they were handling a newborn baby, they carefully laid their friend across the front of the deck. Hickey headed back to the wheel as Winkler closed his eyes and said a silent prayer for his fallen comrade. When he had finished and reopened his eyes, he was looking right at the two unused cinder blocks and chains.

Jenson Cole saw Winkler heft one of the cinder blocks and walk his way.

"Hey, I told you what you wanted to know," Cole protested.

Winkler set the cinder block at Jenson Cole's feet and went back for a chain, deaf to the protest.

"This ain't right!" Cole yelled.

Hickey just watched as Winkler triple-wrapped the chain around the center of the cinder block and started wrapping the chain ends around Jenson Cole's ankles. Jenson Cole couldn't believe this was happening. Not to him! He was the one who disposed of people in the lake. He had thought the soldiers would drop him off at the police or something after they'd picked up Yoder, and he could use his money and influence to command or pay off yet another problem.

"You can't do this to a Cole!" Jenson screamed, as he felt the cold steel wrapped tight and saw Winkler tie the chain ends together in knots until he was satisfied. "It's not part of the deal."

Jeff Winkler hefted the heavy cinder block over the side and let it splash into the water. The weight dragged Cole overboard, but Winkler grabbed his torso and held the man in a viselike grip.

"What were Yoder's final words?" Winkler asked.

Cole thought for a moment. He remembered that night. After he and his men had captured the preacher, savagely beaten and bloodied him, and prepared him for the lake, he still wasn't a broken man.

As Larry Yoder was being prepared to be lowered into the water for a final time, he had looked right at Jenson Cole and smiled. "I forgive you," the former Special Forces man had stated with nothing but truth in his voice. "I forgive all of you, and I love you as brothers." Then the former soldier, now a man of God, had started the Lord's Prayer aloud.

That infuriated Jenson Cole, and it was he who had pushed Yoder off the boat into the water.

Jenson Cole remembered all of that, and still his fury at Yoder's unbreakable will angered him.

"I don't remember," he replied to Winkler's question.

"Did he beg?" Winkler asked, looking deep into Cole's eyes for the truth.

There was a long pause before Cole answered. "Yeah. He whimpered like a dog."

"You're lying," Winkler flatly stated. "Tell you what," he calmly told the man. "I can hold my breath four minutes underwater. But you're so tough I bet you can last eight minutes. You got that long to come back up. That's our deal."

Jenson Cole started to say something, but as he was finding his words Winkler let loose with his right hand, drew it back in a fist, and drove it with all of his might into Jenson Cole's wounded gut. Anything that man wanted to say was overpowered by the air coming out of his lungs as Winkler released his grip and pushed the man away from the boat.

Hickey and Winkler watched a few bubbles rise to the surface where Jenson Cole sank to the bottom. The last thing Cole saw was the two others he had sent down to this very spot.

"Want to stick around?" Hickey asked.

"I said I would," Winkler said. "Eight minutes."

"Why did you push him away like that? He was going down either way."

"Didn't want him to knock himself out hitting the boat," Winkler said pragmatically. "He would miss the complete experience then."

They sat in silence as the minutes ticked by.

"Can I go now?" Hickey asked after ten minutes had passed.

Winkler peered over the side into the still waters.

"Sure. I don't see him here."

The trip back to the dock was quicker and much more solemn. Everyone had held out some small hope that Yoder was still alive and just being kept locked up somewhere. The body in the boat ended any thoughts of that.

However, they had brought their friend and fellow soldier back. Fred Custer had fulfilled his oath.

WHILE HICKEY TIED UP TO the dock, Winkler ran back to the Jeep and told Custer that they had the corpse, grabbed a body bag, then ran back to the boat. He and Hickey gently lowered Larry Yoder into the black bag and zipped it shut. They brought him back to the land and started for the Jeep. Winkler told Hickey to hold on.

They lowered the body bag to the ground, and Winkler went back to the boat for the duffle bag. One final thing was pulled out of it. The tracker set the timer on the C-4 plastic explosive for half an hour and ran back to Hickey. He placed the duffle bag across the top of the body bag, and the two men carried to the Jeep what felt like the heaviest weight either of them had ever lifted.

Hickey and Winkler laid the body in the back of the Jeep after setting the backseat flat. Then all the men changed from camos into civilian clothes and set off for Belle Glade.

They stopped at the Shell station next to the Lion Country Safari where Hickey had tasted a cold bottle of Mexican Coca-Cola long ago. It was late, and the clerk wondered why these men were buying thirty bags of ice as they filled the Jeep's gas tank.

"Big party. An old friend just came home," Hickey explained.

He set three more of the glass bottles of Mexican-made Coke on the counter. The bill was just over ninety dollars.

Hickey slapped a hundred-dollar bill onto the counter.

"Keep the change, kid." He smiled.

The three men and Larry Yoder's body set off on the road back to Vero Beach. Custer popped open the bottled Cokes, and all three men tasted them. About that time, the C4 exploded, and the Cole family bass boat was ripped apart into a thousand shards across the lake.

"Hey, these are better than the cans," Custer noted.

"Told you," Hickey said back.

Once they were on Interstate 95 heading north, the Cokes almost gone, Custer turned to the quiet man in the back with the body.

"Winkler," he said, "just what did you whisper to that guy to make him talk?"

"I told him what I would do to him." Winkler lapsed into silence again.

"And just what would that have been?" Hickey questioned.

Winkler was quiet for a moment.

"I told him that I would spread him naked, roped to stakes out in the sun. Cut his eyelids off so he goes blind." Winkler was quiet for another moment, and then he continued. "Cut a two-inch hole in his side and pull his intestines out. Let the ants crawl on those, biting him."

Hickey and Custer felt holes in their guts thinking about that.

"On the third morning I would bring that two-foot gator to him and watch it bite his balls off. I would use a burning torch to cauterize the wound. Make sure he didn't die. I told him I would make sure it took at least a week for him to die, and that those things were the nice things I would do to him. I told him he could talk now or during that week. And if he waited any time, no matter when he talked, I would finish the week out on him. So he told us. White people scare easy."

"And you could have done all of that to that man?" Custer asked.

"Man? He was no man," Winkler replied. "The Coles were evil spirits walking the earth. I have seen the ghosts of such evil spirits deep in the Superstition Mountains. It was good to rid the earth of them."

The men in the Jeep lapsed back into silence.

"Remind me to never get on your bad side," Custer said.

"Never happen, Fred. Not in this life," Winkler replied. "But I'll tell you this, we white boys were damn lucky there were so few Apache in the Old West."

"I think we were," Custer agreed.

They arrived back at Vero Beach at 4:00 A.M.

Geraldine Custer understood why the man she loved cried in her arms until dawn.

REVEILLE

CHAPTER 23

*Each man should keep a list of tips and lessons learned
and add to them after each operation.*

—POI 7658 Special Forces Combat Manual ROV 1970

Ɪᴛ ᴡᴀs ᴀ ᴄᴏʟᴅ, ɢʀᴀʏ ᴅᴀʏ when Larry Yoder was buried
with reverence in an old family plot on Amish land. After Custer
contacted his father, the old man had suggested that idea. It avoided
many formal questions and explanations to city and county officials
that a burial through a standard funeral, in a public cemetery, would
have brought. Within the quiet Amish community, the Yoder family
had blood relatives whose Luddite ways still kept them away from
the usual required paperwork, autopsies, and questions.

Custer could have easily bought a death certificate to go along
with such an event and prevent further investigation. He had also
checked with Arlington National Cemetery, and the former Special

Forces soldier easily qualified for one of the few remaining spots among the hallowed military dead.

He felt it better to defer to Larry's father, though. As most of Yoder's life had been dedicated to religion, Custer felt this was a fine way to formally bury the body.

The six men who had been on the operation in faraway Florida to recover the body were all in their military uniforms for the event. A couple of them had been let out by a local tailor. Sharkey settled for the only British uniform Custer could locate on such short notice. It was the uniform of a Royal Marine, bought off eBay and FedExed to a tailor in Pennsylvania near the Amish community. Sharkey had never been a Royal Marine, but under the circumstances, he was not picky.

The Amish community had an elders' meeting to agree to the funeral. While Yoder hadn't been one of them, his family roots and his lifelong dedication to God swayed the council. As to the odd request by the military men for a twenty-one-gun salute, the council agreed to that, also.

Custer and the others with him had to borrow a distant cousin of Yoder's to make up the proper seven-man unit to fire the blanks into the air. The man was unsure about firing the old M-1, but after firing the blanks through it the day before, he was at ease the day of the event.

The three seven-round volleys went off as planned and in perfect unison. Hickey gathered the spent brass .30–06 casings while Fred Custer carefully folded the United States flag that had draped over the casket. The flag and empty shell casings were handed over to Larry Yoder's father.

The final prayers were said, and the clean white pine casket was lowered by sturdy ropes into the ground. Larry Yoder had come home for his final rest.

The ex-soldiers all took shovels in hand and piled the cold dirt atop their former comrade in arms, the man who would always be in their hearts and thoughts. Even Fred Custer insisted on being rolled over to the pile of dirt to assist in the final actions.

Afterward, everyone shared in the bountiful table the Amish had prepared. It was a good meal, and everyone spoke of the eloquence and sincerity of the funeral.

By 8:00 P.M., Fred Custer, Geraldine, and almost all of the men were at a private Pittsburgh airport aboard an eight-seat Learjet for the trip back to Vero Beach. Sharkey took the opportunity to head back into Canada. He had buried enough of his mates in his day. Away from his wife, dogs, and cottage long enough, Sharkey wanted to be home now.

He said his good-byes, smiled, and slipped away in a hired limo for his trip back to Niagara Falls. From there he took a public tour bus back into Canada, then to the airport, and from there he crossed the Atlantic back to his home. He missed his cottage with its warm fire and his two dogs lying there as he read. More deeply, he missed his wife, the rock in his life for over twenty years now.

A month later, when the Federal Express deliveryman knocked on his quiet country cottage door, he had no idea why the man was there. When he saw the Vero Beach return address, he signed for and accepted the heavy box, taking it into his office and cutting it open with one of his many knives.

He unwrapped a sturdy red leatherbound edition of Tolstoy's *War and Peace* from the heavily taped bubble wrap around it. He tried opening the book but found that difficult. Sensing something, he sat and studied it as a soft English rain rolled drops down the windows.

Sharkey figured out that the outer boards and page edges were glued shut. Carefully, he took a sharp K-bar knife and cut along the clear bead of dried glue that ran under the top edge of the red leather. When he pried the top cover open, he found the core of the book pages had been cut away. He pulled the heavy cream-colored sheet of Fred Custer's personal stationery off the top and dropped the book when he saw the 25,000 pounds underneath that note.

He stared at the money in the book on the floor.

He had not asked for any payment. The subject had never come up, and it was certainly not why he had gone to Florida. He read the note written in Fred Custer's flowing script.

> It was a pleasure meeting you. I hope you enjoy the book and accept it in the spirit in which it is given. May the inner pages bring you happiness and keep you healthy, wealthy, and wise for a long time. Contact me anytime.
>
> FRED CUSTER

That December, he was curious as he opened the Christmas card that arrived from Florida. It contained no money, but the warmest wishes from Fred and Geraldine for the coming year.

Sharkey didn't know it yet, but he had become one of the Custer faithful.

BACK IN VERO BEACH, CUSTER, Hickey, Hargis, Winkler, and Hadad relaxed on the beach.

They had already taken a trip on John Sterling's boat and dumped almost everything connected with the misson deep into the swells of the Atlantic Ocean. There was only one thing connected to them that was not thrown overboard in the middle of the night thirty miles from shore.

It took the promise of a brand-new, custom-built Barrett .50 caliber rifle to get Hargis to dump the sniper's rifle overboard. The rest stood back, Hargis's back to them, as he whispered to the rifle. Only John Sterling thought the sight odd.

Van Zandt, the quiet man from Orlando, was paid to handle the Jeep and Land Rover that had been purchased. He paid two trustworthy men to drive the cars from Orlando across the southern states and deep into Texas. A week after the operation those two trucks were driven into the Mexican border town of Nuevo Laredo.

The two men walked away from the vehicles, keys left in the ignitions and the doors unlocked, and took a bus back across the border into Laredo. From there they took commercial flights to Houston and then back to Orlando.

The former Special Forces soldiers enjoyed their time together. They swam in the still warm waters. They had long dinners speaking of their time together and their lives since Vietnam.

One night they broke out the cards and chips and began an all-night poker game. When Fred got out the serious Cuban cigars, Geraldine spoke up.

She didn't mind the occasional one Fred smoked, but there was no way she was having five men, playing cards for God knows how long, stink up her house with that odor. The men, who had numerous times faced death from the Viet Cong and the North Vietnamese Army, moved the game out onto the porch. The five hardened warriors, the men who had broken the Cole family's back and left it bleeding in the dirt to die, knew when they were beaten. They had all had a good woman in their lives.

Smiling, Geraldine kept sandwiches, beer, and snacks on the table all night. Winkler proved as deft at poker as he was at moving through the brush silently. The chips piled up in front of him.

Geraldine joined the game at 2:00 A.M. She cut Winkler's chips in half before they called it a night. Fred Custer learned something new about his wife of twenty years.

Over the next few days, the men started taking off for their homes again. Dan Hadad was the first to go. He had used all of his vacation time, and it was time to see his wife again, to put this adventure behind him and return to a tie-bound nine-to-five.

Hargis, grinning as he hugged each man, took off on a Tuesday morning in one of Custer's hired jets, his guitar in tow. Instead of Beaumont, his next stop was Murfreesboro, Tennessee, home of Barrett Firearms, to get his new custom-made .50 caliber rifle.

Winkler drove north back toward Atlanta, where his loving wife and beautiful child waited.

The night after Winkler left, Fred, Geraldine, and Hickey enjoyed another crab dinner at Vero Beach's best restaurant. They went to sleep late and had Hickey at the private airport at noon. The private charter was happy to wait while the three said their good-byes.

"Well, we did it, Hickey," Fred said.

"Yes, we did," Hickey replied. "I wish we hadn't been forced to."

"We did what had to be done. Hard as that was." Fred paused, then went on. "But it had to be done."

"I know, Fred."

The two men shook hands, Geraldine kissed Hickey on the cheek, and he turned and waved as he reached the top step of the jet. The door closed, and they waved and smiled again after Hickey had settled into a thick leather seat and looked back to the Custers through the window.

Fred and Geraldine Custer didn't leave until the jet had flown away and was out of sight.

Each of the men left with fifty thousand dollars—the same amount the British soldier had received. None of them wanted it. All of them protested and tried to hand it back.

"Think of it as a tribute to Larry Yoder," Custer responded to them all. "Use it as you want. Give it away. But it's something I can afford. What we did cannot be bought."

They all took the money.

THE SURVIVING HIRED COLE MEN were all brought to trial. With the Cole family destroyed, the workers who had suffered under their injustices came forth and testified against them all.

An anonymous note was delivered to Officer Jackson, and the lake bottom was searched. Twenty-seven bodies and skeletons were brought up, some going back decades. Many missing person cases were closed; families got final closure, and more funerals were held.

Three of the survivors went to Raiford State Prison to wait on death row. All the rest got long sentences and didn't fare well behind the walls, where racist ethnic gangs were more than happy to take their anger out on the white prisoners who were not protected by the white gangs. The just-as-racist white gangs did nothing to protect these unknown men. One by one, they were cut down in the unseen corners and dark cells where the prison guards knew better than to roam. The three men on death row were the only ones who lasted more than a year.

They were protected from the gangs, but nothing stopped their sentences from being carried out.

BELLE GLADE CHANGED WITH THE Coles gone. The chief of police and his two top men also went to prison. Like the others within the general population, they didn't last long. Ex–police officers, no matter what their crimes, were prime targets for the rough prisoners.

The large international corporate farming interests swooped down onto Belle Glade like vultures onto a carcass. The life of the average cane worker didn't improve much under the tenure of the uncaring corporate structures, but the beatings and killings stopped.

The surviving Cole women and children knew they didn't stand a chance of running the operation. There were too many indictments; too many bodies were brought up from under the lake.

They took what they could get for the land and houses and disappeared from Belle Glade and tried to resettle in places where they were not known.

Nevertheless, the legacy of their kin followed them wherever they went. Poppa Cole's legacy was blood and death, and the stain of it was like ink spilled on a white dress. A person can wash it out somewhat, but it never truly goes away.

Each time they moved and thought they were far enough away, it didn't take long for the local press and TV cameras to come knocking at their doors. The story had gone national, and no matter where a Cole family member moved, reporters were waiting to bite.

They never figured out that those reporters all received fat envelopes of newspaper clippings and DVDs of the South Florida TV news shows. All the envelopes were postmarked from Orlando. Many of the reporters tried to contact the sender, but those attempts always ran into a dead end.

A FEW MONTHS AFTER EVERYTHING had calmed down, Officer Jackson was waiting for dinner when there was a knock at his door. His wife was busy in the kitchen as he opened it.

The quiet man from Orlando told him that he was there "as a representative of the man at the gas pump." They went outside to talk.

Van Zandt handed Jackson a metal box with twenty-five thousand dollars in cash in it. On top was a business card with a telephone number and "for emergency only" written on it.

"I can't take money for that," Jackson flatly stated.

"Give it to charity," Van Zandt said, walking away. "But if it were me, I would turn it into gold and silver and bury it. You're a young man, Jackson. You never know when something like that will come in handy. I've been around a long time. You never know what happens down the road."

Jackson was very quiet around the house the next three days. His wife was almost worried. He finally decided that the stranger's advice was not bad, and he drove to Miami on his next off-duty day.

Never buying more than three thousand dollars at any one coin shop, he converted most of the paper into metal. He kept five thousand dollars in bills and buried the box deep in his backyard.

Van Zandt was right. One never knew what the future might bring, and a little secret stash might just come in handy one day.

FRED AND GERALDINE CUSTER SETTLED back into their rhythms by the beach. They started recirculating among their friends in Vero Beach and going back to their lives before the operation.

When they were asked where they had been, they would reply "Oh, we were busy on a project," and somehow move the conversation away from the nature of their actions during the past couple of months.

One night, on the patio, as they were entertaining another couple they knew, the woman guest pointed over to something by the side of the sliding glass door. It didn't fit the decor and hardly seemed right among the tasteful patio furniture.

"That wasn't here before. Where did you get it?" she asked, pointing.

"That?" Fred commented. "That came from an old friend." And the conversation moved on to the northern snowbird tourists who were starting to fill Vero Beach again.

Sitting on the wooden deck by the sliding glass doors, stood a simple cement cinder block with a piece of chain wrapped around the center support. Whenever he saw it, Fred Custer was reminded of his many friends.